MW01204513

Your friend —
Rit
7-20-10

The Little White House

And Other Short Stories

By

Richard W Anderson

ISBN 0-7414-5699-0

Published by:

INFI∞ITY
PUBLISHING.COM

1094 New DeHaven Street, Suite 100
West Conshohocken, PA 19428-2713
Info@buybooksontheweb.com
www.buybooksontheweb.com
Toll-free (877) BUY BOOK
Local Phone (610) 941-9999
Fax (610) 941-9959

Printed in the United States of America

Published March 2010

With gratitude to my editors:

Gilbert Anderson
Billy Davis

and

Appreciation to my wife
Lee Anderson and my daughter
Christine Stolz for their
love and encouragement.

The Stories

The Little White House

Though it was the depression era the Lundstrum family farm was functioning very near normal—mom, dad and two boys. Then one summer day the boys encounter a burly red-haired stranger from "here, there, and everywhere" who for a break in his travels squats on their farm and subsequently captivates the boys with his tales of travel and adventure. Which stories are true and which fiction? The boys are enthralled with this presumed life of daring and adventure, but as well could the stranger be enlightened by the boys happy lives compared to his own as a vagabond.

The Great Indian Raid of 1910

Gib was a precocious farm lad who became intrigued by the locals' stories about the days when the Kansa Indians thrived on the very prairie on which his family now farmed and raised mules. There were still occasional real, or imagined, sightings of Indians who some thought still mindful of recouping their ancestral lands. Gib couldn't help but ponder—what would the consequences be if an Indian raiding party were to invade the little town of Partridge in one terrifying evening? He was determined to find out.

Skippy's Short Summer

A little pup arrives unexpectedly on the Kansas farm. Through clever antics he quickly ingratiates himself to the entire farm clan and is accepted as a resident. It soon becomes evident that he had been a "city dog" and unaccustomed to the inherent hazards of farm life. He tangles with the "fighting rooster," the barnyard bull, ant

hills, bull snakes and other prairie hazards. In spite of all
of the pups tribulations he brings joy to all those around
him and ultimately also teaches others a life's lesson in
loving and respecting one another while having the
opportunity.

Escape from Babylon

Two teenage boys have summer jobs in the 50's as
busboys at an upscale St. Louis supper club. One evening
after getting off work they ill-advisedly decide to make a
late night trek over the Mississippi to the then infamous
East St. Louis to visit a couple of jazz clubs. One stop led
to another and they ultimately found themselves in a
house of ill repute where things didn't go quite as things
are ordinarily expected to go in such establishments.
What transpired was not likely to be soon forgotten by the
boys, the "lady", nor the establishment proprietor.

The Christmas Coin

Times were tough in the Mueller household. Dad lost his
job at the local hardware when Wal-Mart moved to town.
Mom was a "stay at home mom" and son Bill worked part
time at the NEWS DEPOT to help out with household
expense. Though times were lean the love in the home
was abundant. Bill's fortuitous on the job discovery of a
rare coin promised to have a dramatic effect on the lives
of the Mueller family and coincidentally on the proprietor
of the NEWS DEPOT as well.

The Elevator Incident

It seemed an ordinary day 'til the elevator in the Bradley
Building got stuck between floors with six people aboard.
The six had various personal profiles and reacted to their
dilemma in totally, and in some cases, unexpected ways.
There was the frustrated salesman, the woman and her un-

wanted pregnancy, the rock solid widow, and the others who all somehow found the commonality of being captives the time to vent their personal situations to perfect strangers. Consequently by the time they exited the elevator, after three hours together, they were no longer strangers and perhaps even a bit wiser.

Charlie's Letter

While serving during the Korean War Bill Andrews and Company are on a frozen battlefield retreating from marauding Chinese when fleeing to the rear he literally stumbles over a dying soldier. The soldier, taking his last breaths, finds the strength to pass along a letter he'd written to his sweetheart, implying his hope for ultimate delivery.

Andrews takes the letter with no clear intent as to disposition. Some months later his business takes him near the addressed town and he makes a side trip to try and find the addressee. He finds the young woman, delivers the letter, and the impact on both their lives is dramatic and lasting.

Western Military Caper

They were high school guys in the 50's that hung together who had a club—The Eight Balls. Dandy, the neat as a mannequin Eight Ball, was victim of an up-grading in environment when his mother decided he would be better off attending military school than be associated with the Eight Balls. The boys missed their friend and one Friday night, five of them, decided to pay Dandy a visit. They drove to the military school, located Dandy's barracks, and soon thereafter stealth turned to bedlam. With night watchmen, and city police, in pursuit, the five Eight Balls managed a safe retreat to their home turf, only to discover later, they really didn't get away with it.

Lessons Learned

Paul Stover was supportive of civic causes and was a member of the Bluecoats, an organization benefiting the children of police officers. As was his practice he attended the Bluecoats annual dinner and mingled with his peers and law enforcement officers. Driving from the dinner he was stopped by a police officer who suspected Paul was D.U.I. and he in fact failed the testing. Taken to the station Paul made the allowable phone call to his attorney for help and in the interim they put him in the "tank" with others awaiting action. Paul was subjected to the incredulous stories of his cell-mates which ranged from humorous, to scary, to pathetic.

Heaven—In Time

Marty had the task of shoveling the snow off his walk and driveway. A sharp pain down his left arm, a belt to the chest, and he collapses. His wife immediately calls 911. EMS promptly respond and deliver Marty to EMERGENCY. One moment on the ER table and the next moment Marty finds himself arriving in Heaven. He soon encounters his "acclimator" who welcomes him and gives him a rundown on what to expect. Once acclimated Marty meets up with biblical and historic figures and does his time in "enlightenment" sessions. He has some surprises while learning of some facets of the after-life he never would have expected. The biggest surprise was his final destination.

Contents

The Little White House

I never did have a firm understanding as to the origin of the "little white house". I just knew it had stood, or leaned, there abandoned as far back as I could remember. We lived on the flatlands of South Central Kansas. The family's original 160 acre homestead was a few miles west, and when this 320 acre place became available in 1910 because of a death or two, my grandfather sold the original farm, did some horse trading, visited the state bank, moved and doubled his acreage and prospered. The "little white house" at the new place was thought to probably have been the original homesteader's home and my grandfather with a wife and three sons would have needed and built a little larger home, perhaps better situated on the land.

When my mother and father married my grandfather gave way to them in 1920 and he and my grandmother moved to a nearby town, or in a word were put to pasture, and my father took over the farming. Legacy-wise made easy as neither of my dad's younger brothers were interested in farming and both had gone on to find good jobs and settle in Wichita. My dad, Bill, was a pleasant fellow with a wry sense of humor and though occasionally somewhat stern, a loving father. He was of medium physical stature though among the farmer class that could be misleading; he was as strong as a bull and on occasion proved same to the bull.

Mom, Ruth, farm-raised just down the road a piece from Dad, was a pretty black haired woman with very precise facial features—high cheek bones, sharp ridged nose and expressive brown eyes. As with most farm women of the times she was extraordinarily hardworking, whether cooking, sewing, canning or scooping wheat alongside the men folk, while at the same time was very gentle and loving to her family, and helpful to her neighbors.

My brother Ben was eighteen months older than me and though more brassy and wiry than me, we got along pretty good. In fact, he kinda looked out for his little brother whether it was a prospective problem we might have with Dad or a bullying schoolmate. We were best friends.

The "little white house" was about a quarter mile east

down the dusty road from our home on the pastures edge in a cluster of cottonwood trees. A cottonwood grove was unusual on the Kansas prairie and it was surmised it got there as part of the Homestead Act which had a provision that if the Homesteader put in X number of trees he'd get a bonus of so many acres in addition to the base 160. Thus, our farm had a cottonwood grove of about 15 acres as part of the pasture. The cottonwoods were as straight as candy cane averaging about thirty feet tall, about half way to their probable final height. During the early summer the fluffy cotton seeds float from the trees like summer snow and in the fall the leaves turn bright yellow before falling and carpeting the grove floor. A tornado had come through and taken a lot of the cottonwoods down (as well as the barn roof) which made for some timber clutter, and cow path obstacles, but for a kid it gave us lots of fallen trees to romp on and around.

The "little white house" wasn't really "white" any longer. It was a faded white blotched aged gray wood clapboard house, with a little windward tilt, about 25 foot by 25 foot with a crawl space beneath and a wood, shingle here shingle there, gable roof. The interior was split into three necessarily small rooms. The larger room had a brick chimney apparently for a cooking stove and a Franklin heating stove and the other two rooms were small probably intended sleeping rooms. No plumbing of course. The interior walls and ceiling were wood lath and plaster though now mostly exposed aged gray lath. Oddly, though numerous cracks, most of the glass windows were in tact as were the floor boards and exterior doors. There was a trap door to an attic neither Ben nor I ever had built the courage to explore—one never knows. A nearby stream sometimes ran by the "little white house"; sometimes because if there were long Kansas dry spells the stream bed was likewise. There must have been a well and outhouse at one time but any evidence of either was long gone. A cow path from the barnyard wound several hundred feet through the cottonwoods along by the "little white house" and on to the main grassy cow pasture. Ben and I would often make the trek along the path with no particular destination in mind but as we approached the creepy old house something invariably drew us to stop and peek inside, but nothing could ever entice us to that darned attic door. We could certainly have figured a way to boost one or the other up to get an attic peek, but it never happened.

One summer day our lives took a turn we wouldn't soon forget. It was mid-afternoon when Ben suggested we go see what action we could stir up out in the cottonwood grove. It was always fun to balance walk a downed tree, see how big a sheet of dead bark we could peel off a downed cottonwood to use later in building a camp-out lean-to or just stir up a cottontail or two or maybe a bull snake. We'd been having rain so there was water in the creek too in case we got the urge to go skinny-dipping.

Ben saw it first. "There's smoke over by the 'little white house'."

"My gosh, you're right—there is."

A narrow line of gray smoke was twisting skyward about 100 yards over.

Ben said, "We better take a look."

"Yea," I agreed.

We headed double-time towards the spiraling gray smoke. As we got to within about 200 feet we saw movement alongside the house. We went from double-time to a crouched over caterpillar-like creeping.

"What is this?" Ben said.

"Don't know. We better find out," I responded.

We were now flat-out on our bellies snaking towards the smoke; we were close now. Then we saw HIM! There stood a man the likes of which we'd never seen before. He was well over six foot tall, with flaming red hair and matching mustache and short red beard. He wore a red and black checkered hunter's shirt, a leather vest, what looked like heavy-duty dark blue denim trousers, held up by leather suspenders, and what must have been size fifteen leather boots. His shoulders were as broad as a bridge. He was a BIG man. At this point he apparently heard our commotion in the brush.

"WHO GOES THERE!?," he roared. Ben and I were on our bellies a couple feet apart and I swear I could feel the ground beneath quivering from his thunderous inquiry.

He HAD us!

"Stand up you two! What are you doing sneaking up on a fella like that?" he boomed. Thunder, in a word, he rocked us like thunder. And he wanted to know what WE were doing here.

"Com'on outta there!"

We raised our trembling bodies, I moved to Ben's backside as I was wont to do in that kind of crisis, and we took an ever few slow steps towards this intruding giant of a man. "We live over there—this is our cow pasture and we are just playing around," Ben said rather timidly.

The giant said, "Oh, OK come over here boys," a little more friendly like. "What names you go by?"

"I'm Ben and this is my little brother Richard."

"You boy's gotta last name?"

"Yes sir—Lundstrom."

He now lowered his voice another octave and said, "My name's William Wallace, but you lads can call me Rusty." He held out a big freckled right hand that Ben hesitantly took as Rusty firmly over-gripped with his other hand and pumped Ben's arm. I planted my feet and stretched an arm to a finger tip shake which Rusty accommodated while looking at me rather peculiarly. Thank the Lord he had a smile on his face.

He said, "You boys wanna go over there and sit a spell?" as he motioned towards the house and two cottonwood logs he'd arranged opposite one another on the ground, about six feet between, with a stone fire ring in the middle around a few glowing embers.

Ben said, "Sure," as we, still clearly apprehensive, walked over and squatted on a log, as he squatted opposite.

"You boys say you live around here," he asked.

"Yes sir," I said, "just over yonder a little ways. Our daddy farms this place and this here's our pasture."

Rusty asked, "And what does your daddy raise on this here farm?"

"Mostly wheat," Ben said, "some alfalfa for the cows, some oats."

"No corn?" Rusty asked.

"No sir, not much corn grown around here, too dry," Ben responded.

"Got a garden," he asked.

"Yes sir, a big garden with tomatoes, green beans and taters," Ben said.

"Good to know."

"What's that?"

"Never mind," and he went on, "hard to believe just a hundred or so miles south and west of here the farms have turned to dust and folks are loading up and heading far west."

I spoke up, "Over along the road there's lots of sand-hill plum bushes too; all you can eat, but stay away from the green ones they'll give you a belly ache."

Ben had the courage, not me, to ask, "And where are you from Mr. Rusty?"

"Here there and everywhere."

"Oh—where are you going?"

"Here there and everywhere."

"Oh."

With that his white teeth popped out through that red beard and he broke into a wide grin; on closer look I could see that one of his two front teeth was missing. That remaining was pearly white. He poked the red embers with a stick. By now I felt pretty sure he wasn't going to harm us.

Mr. Rusty said, "Do you think your daddy would mind if I hung around for a few days? I've been walking and hopping freights for a couple weeks and I'd sure like to rest a spell, my bones are begging for a break."

Ben took it upon himself to speak for Dad, "No I don't think he'd care, you aint hurtin' nothin'." Just the same I thought we better run this by Dad, but kept quiet for now.

"Good," Rusty said. "I've got a bedroll in that little ole

house and find it right comfortable. Who's house was it anyway?" He'd about poked the fire out by now.

I spoke up, "We really don't know for sure who built it or why it's here. My daddy thinks it was probably the house the first family that farmed this here land built a long time ago."

Rusty said, "You mean you don't know who lived in that house or what might have gone on in there?"

"No sir," I said.

"Why you're right on the trail between Kansas City and Dodge City. Wyatt Earp himself could have stopped by here, or Wild Bill maybe on his way to Dodge. Boy, if only those old walls could talk. You know not many years ago there were lots of renegade Indians rampaging through this territory. Why an hombre could have been scalped right there where you sit!"; as he swished a hand knife-like over his red head. Then with one eyebrow arched, "Ever see any ghost signs around here, you know like sights or sounds you can't explain."

"Not really, but I'll tell you this, we aint never lifted the trap door to that attic in there," Ben said.

"Can't blame you for that," Rusty said.

Rusty asked, "Have you ever checked to see if there are any unsolved murders in this county? Probably ought to do that; you never know."

I'd heard all I could absorb and besides it was time to go home for lunch and Ben and I had some afternoon chores and then milking to do. I spoke up, "Ben we better be getting home and tend to our chores."

Ben said, "Yea, OK, will you be here later Mr. Rusty?"

"I told you boys if your daddy doesn't have a problem I thought I might stick around and rest for a few days; I'm right comfortable here."

"OK."

Ben and I took the cow path home. Mom fixed us some lunch and had already taken Dad's to him in the field to shorten his down time from plowing. We quite casually told Mom about meeting Rusty and that he was from here there and everywhere. We didn't get much reaction. After lunch we had garden chores and after I grabbed the egg bucket to gather the eggs and Ben went to the milk barn and fetched and poured wheat bran in the cow trough for the cows milking eats. Like clockwork, around five, the cows and their companion heifers, steers, and the sole bull, that Dad named Lucky, made their way from the pasture to the barnyard where the cows filed into the barn for the bran for milk exchange while the other livestock munched on the alfalfa Ben had pitched into the barnyard feeder. Besides Lucky the bull only the milking cows had names. Dad said if we were gonna pull on a cows privates twice a day we oughta at least know their names; Mom didn't think that was funny.

Milking and chores done it was time for dinner where that evening Mom dished out her, better than most could make, chicken and dumplings. While eating Ben and I eyed each other apprehensively—who was going to bring up the subject of Rusty? I began slowly, inconspicuously, bobbing my head in Ben's direction suggesting, go-ahead, go-ahead. Ben knowing it was to be his lead, said, "How was your day Dad?"

"Why my day was fine son—OK let's have it, what have you guys done now?"

Mom said, "Now Daddy."

Dad said, "OK, let's have it."

"We didn't do nothing, but there's something you probably oughta know about," Ben said.

"What's that?"

"Well," Ben went on, "a man, a real nice man, a really big man, is sorta stopping over down at the 'little white house'."

"A nice man is stopping over! What'a'ya mean a nice man is stopping over—what'a we running here, a tourist court?"

Fortunately Mom chimed in, "Now Daddy, you know as well as I do that in these times they're lots of men finding their way across this here country looking for a life, or at least some work. I'll remind you that over the past several weeks I've fed three travelin' men right from that back door. They were hungry and I, we, fed them. Don't get yourself all worked up because one of these poor souls rests here for a few days in that broken down old house that I've been trying to get you to tear down for years."

Dad, smiling, "Are you through old woman?"

Mom, "Yes, and don't call me old woman."

Dad said, "We don't want any squatters around here, but if he's just passing through I guess it's OK."

Once again Mom demonstrated her wise counsel and influence.

The next morning Ben and I rolled out of bed a little earlier than usual, slipped into our overalls, rushed through our chores of milking and filling the chicken feeder and found our way to the breakfast table. Dad had already had his vegetable-sized bowl full of oatmeal and four eggs, bacon, toast and jam, hot coffee, and was already out on the John Deere plowing the north field. Ben and I had some bacon and scrambled eggs, and tomato juice. We were a in little bit of a hurry, gulped down our food, and soon pushed our chairs back from the table and started for the back door.

Mom hollered, "Hold it a minute you two, I know where you're going—here take this to our visitor," and handed us a paper bag. We peeked inside the bag and saw it held two buttered biscuits, several pieces of crisp bacon, and a not to easy to come by, orange. That was our Mom.

Ben and I raced to the path to the pasture as we heard a fading "Be back for lunch" over our shoulders. We approached the "little white house" and saw no sign of life around the house. Ben said, "Do you suppose he's gone?"

"I don't know, let's look inside."

We went to the closest door and cautiously entered the spooky house to find Rusty was there alright sitting in a corner, leaning against the wall, reading a book. I couldn't catch the title of the book, but could see it was sure used looking. His bedroll was open on the floor, a small backpack, and a little tin box alongside. The box looked like a tin that maybe held flour, or sugar or something like that, but I couldn't tell because the print was scratched and faded. Wedged between exposed lath were a couple of pictures— one appeared to have been torn from a magazine and was of a pretty smiling lady in a swimming costume with her back to the camera peeking over her shoulder with one hand on her hip and the other holding an umbrella over head. The other picture looked like a snapshot and was of a real pretty girl sitting atop a picnic table with a lake in the background; there was some writing on the pictures white border, but I couldn't make it out.

We didn't ask.

"Well good morning my two farm fed lads and how are you two this fine beautiful Kansas morning? Boys I've never been in Kansas before; don't that wind ever stop? It's hot, but it ain't hot. I'll tell you another thing, laying in here at night listening to that wind blowin' through them cotton-woods sounds like God leading a symphony. It's truly soothing, inspiring; gets ya' to thinking about life."

Ben said, "That may be, but if you stay around here long enough you'll hear that wind sound more like God driving a freight train through them cottonwoods."

Rusty added, "You know what else—if I could truly paint them golden blue sunsets you got out here I'd be a rich man, yes sir, and see that patch of sunflowers over yonder? At sun-up with the morning dew glistening atop them bright yellow brown belly-buttoned flowers, I saw a Van Gogh."

"Van go?"

"Yea, a Van Gogh."

I moved on, "We have a breakfast treat for you," and handed him the paper bag.

He opened it slowly as if he wanted a surprise to sneak up on him. "Oh boy!, B and B, biscuits and bacon, my favorite, and an orange for desert. Thank you boys, and I suspect your momma deserves a thanks too."

Rusty scarfed down the B and B and peeled the orange with a pocket knife so perfectly that when he set the peelings on the floor it looked like an uncut fresh orange.

Ben said, "Daddy said it's OK if you stay around for a few days to rest."

I said, "Mom said it first."

Rusty, "Well that's good news."

Then he said, "Richard, it is Richard isn't it?"

"Yes sir."

"Richard I see you always looking at my mouth. I first thought it was my mustache, but then it hit me, it's this dang old gap aint it? You're wondering, was there ever a tooth there or did I just come this a'way." As he fingered the hole in his upper gum.

"No sir," I said, "I hadn't noticed."

Rusty said, "Well boys I'm a 'gonna tell you about that thar tooth that ain't there. Let's go outside and squat a spell."

We went outside and planted ourselves on the logs he'd laid out the day before. It was morning, but already too hot for a fire. Nonetheless Rusty picked up a stick and began poking the fire rings spent ashes. Rusty was now skipping the vest and long sleeve shirt and just wore a gray undershirt under his suspenders, biceps bulging atop red fuzzy arms.

"Well listen in now boys. I'm sure you guys have heard of a boxer named Jack Dempsey. He came from not too far from here, Manassa, Colorado. They called him 'The Manassa Mauler'. You know it's told he had Choctaw Indian blood in 'im and you better believe it. When a young man he went looking for money fights in saloons. It's said he'd go into a saloon and bellow 'I can sing and I can dance, but I can lick any S.O.B. in the house!' And he generally did, lick anyone in the house that is.

"Well, he went east hopeful to become a big time boxer and in fact before long was beating everybody with the courage to get into the ring with him. His ego, and wallet, were getting pretty big too and he was living the high life with motorcars, women, song and everything that goes with it. In 1919 he got a crack at the big one—heavyweight champion Jess Willard and wouldn't you know it he

12

pulverized Willard. Dempsey was champ and life was real good for several years. Then in 1926 he fought an ex-marine named Gene Tunney in Philadelphia and Tunney up and beat 'im.

"Dempsey was determined to let the world know he wasn't finished and in July 1927 he came back with a fight against a guy named Jack Sharkey and he beat Sharkey, but in an unpopular decision. You see in the late rounds Sharkey was beating Dempsey and Dempsey was clearly hitting Sharkey below the belt and when Sharkey turned to complain to the referee a Dempsey left hook knocked Sharkey cold. Dempsey's victorious arm was raised high by the referee. Well then came the booing, fans on their feet throwing junk into the ring. But, the win over Sharkey entitled him to another crack at Tunney.

"Now boy's, you gotta be thinking, what's this got to do with my missing front tooth—well, just hold on.

"I happened to be in the New York area at that time in my wanderings and saw a little item in the sports section of the New York Post that said the Dempsey crew was looking for sparring partners and to me the money sounded mighty good. I had done some boxing in the Marines several years before so I got my thumb a pumpin' and found my way out'a the city to Dempsey's training camp over in Jersey. Once there I made inquiry and one of his trainers took a look at me and, though I fibbed a little about my boxing background, I guess he liked my size, easier target I suppose, and they took me on. I spent a couple days just loafing around and eating pretty good food, at least by my recent standards, and watching Dempsey used a bunch of big oafs for punching bags.

"Day three was to be my turn to spar with the Manassa Mauler, or perhaps for him to simply pulverize another stooge on his path to fight condition. The day came and maybe not to smart I showed up on schedule at the make-shift arena for a crack at Jack. A trainer handed me, and I put on, a ratty pair of I think once blue boxing trunks, a strap-on leather pad for my groin, a little strip of leather for a mouth protector, and a little padded leather headpiece. On top of everything else you had'ta continuously pinch your nose because the whole place smelled like dirty socks.

"Then Dempsey and crew strutted into the barn and he clearly had that ready-for-the-kill expression on his face. I tell you boys he was ornery looking, like maybe a Choctaw on the war path. There were a couple dozen or so fight hangers-on in the barn arena who apparently relished the sight of someone else's blood. Dempsey nodded in my direction with what I took as a who cares attitude. I was never even introduced to the man. Somebody said let's get to it and some guy took me by the arm and led me towards the ring where he grabbed a pair of stained wrinkled leather gloves that looked awful light weight to me, pulled my arms outright and slipped on and tied the gloves, jammed that leather thing into my mouth, and pushed me towards the ring.

"Dempsey was already in the ring doing a little light fantastic dance—showing off. A trainer told me to remember that this was just a workout and that Dempsey was going to work on his left jab. I told him just a workout was fine with me as someone spread the ropes and I climbed into the ring and probable annihilation.

"We centered ring, touched gloves, somebody hit a bell and he started that dancing business and jabbin' and jabbin' and I was takin' and takin'. I tried to deliver a few jabs myself but mostly just swished air. We went at it for a few minutes with him chasing me around the ring, but to feel like I'd earned my money and with the hope I'd get another go or two at it, the money you know, I really worked at trying not to back away too much and did manage a few glancing blows. Though I was tiring he seemed to gather wind and suddenly he hit me right in the mouth with a wicked right cross. My knees buckled, I was going down, but as I was sinking something gave me a sudden burst of energy and just as a trainer called to Jack, and as Jack turned his head in the direction of the voice, my knees straightened and I came up with a right uppercut straight to his jaw and his eyes popped wide; Jack fell over backwards and hit the ring floor with a thud. He was out cold!

"Well boy's, what was I to do? Several guys jumped in the ring and went to work on Jack with a water bucket, sponge, smelling salts and a couple fanning towels. I stood there in the ring, dumb-struck, thinking, they'll tare me apart, when a man in a suit and tie and fedora motioned me over to the side, took me by the arm and led me out'a the ring towards the door. He told me to get whatever I came with, handed me an extra twenty-five dollars, told me to get the hell out of there, and if I ever told anybody about what happened there, he'd have me killed.

"I got those gloves and groin protector off and as I spit out the leather mouth guard a bloody front tooth came with it; off with the trunks, on with my travelin' clothes, out'a the camp and I thumbed my way back to the city one tooth light but fifty dollars richer and most importantly to me, I had knocked out Jack Dempsey, 'The Manassas Mauler'; only if I told anybody about it I'd be killed.

"So there you have it boy's. That's how I lost that front tooth."

Ben and me, mouths agape, in unison, "WOW!"

Rusty said, "I told you my name was William Wallace didn't I? Do you know what that means?"

"No, not exactly," I responded.

"Boys I'm a Scott and the greatest, bravest, man that ever lived was a Scott named William Wallace, my namesake— known as Braveheart. He ran the English out'a Scotland almost single-handedly along about 1300; well he actually led an army of rag-tag Scots that ran the English out of Scotland. And boys I've got his red blood running through my veins at this very moment. What's you boy's bloodline?"

"Well," Ben said, "Dads a Swede and Mom's a Scott."

"Hmmm," Rusty said, "I guess that makes for peace loving warriors."

I believed his story with all my heart, but really wanted to know, "Whatever happened to Jack Dempsey?"

"Well," Rusty said, "Dempsey re-fought Tunney all right, late in '27, and he knocked Tunney down in the 7th round, but under a new rule Dempsey didn't go to his neutral corner fast enough which gave Tunney an extra five seconds to come around. So Tunney got to his feet before he was counted out and came back and beat Dempsey by decision. Now from the time Tunney went down 'til he got up was 15 seconds which means, boys, if Dempsey had backed off like he shoulda Tunney would have been counted out at ten and Jack would have been champion again. Didn't happen. Which boys I guess means you better know and play by the rules if you expect to win."

Ben spoke up, "We gotta go, Mom told us to be home by noon, maybe we'll be back later."

"Anytime boys, anytime."

"I picked up a few things in Partridge at Puckett's I G A; I'm just fine." I think he picked up a few things from our garden too.

The little town of Partridge was north about two and a half miles if you walked the section roads, but if you walked as a rabbit runs through the pasture and wheat field it was only about a mile. The town's Main north ended at a grain elevator and the Santa Fe line, hardware store, school, grocery, two churches, a few other stores and about 250 hardy folks anchored with a grain elevator and the Rock Island line at Main south.

Ben and I headed for home and some lunch. Dad was washing up outside at the water pump as we got to the house and we did likewise before we all went in and sat down for some chicken noodle soup and cold cuts. Mom said, "The boy's visited with the fella at the 'little white house' this morning."

"And what's he up to, or down to?" Dad asked.

Ben reported, "He knocked out Jack Dempsey."

"WHAT!" I think that noodle that flew across the table

16

traveled through Dad's nose.

"That's it, he's outta here! The guy's a lyin' fraud. He told you boy's he knocked out Jack Dempsey?"

I said, "Yea Dad, he really did. It was kinda an accident, but he did," and gave Dad a brief re-cap of the story.

Dad said, "I don't believe it, not for a minute, when's he movin' on?"

Mom said, as she patted Dad's wrist, "Now Daddy, it could have happened the way they say, it's possible."

Dad retorted, "Yea, about as possible as him striking out Babe Ruth—NO, don't tell me."

I didn't, and neither did Ben, tell Dad about the Wallace guy in Scotland that Rusty shared blood with. He probably wouldn't have believed it.

Dad said, "Well, I'll tell you this much is fact; you boy's got a few jobs to do around here rather than listen to the fantasies of a travelin' flim-flam man. You know there's some fence that needs mending in the south pasture and that chicken house hasn't been cleaned out in a couple months; even the chickens don't like going in there—let's get to it."

Ben and I finished lunch, excused ourselves, and headed for the shop and got a hammer and nails and the wire stretcher for the fence job and a bucket, a rake and scoop shovel for the lousy chicken house job and reluctantly moved on, but we both agreed, tomorrow's another day.

The next morning Ben and I hurriedly ate our breakfast, jumped up quickly to get the milking and our other chores done. I had to check the water level of the cattle tank and either crank on or off the windmill pump and Ben had to run down a plump rooster and be-head same for our dinner. Fortunately plucking the feathers off the carcass was woman's work. We both tended to the chicken feeder and their water trough.

We then went back to tell Mom we were going out to the grove to play around a bit and she intuitively said, "Here's a couple things for your friend," and handed me a paper bag in which a peek revealed a couple hardboiled eggs and an apple. We took the cow path to the cottonwood grove in route to the "little white house". As we approached we saw no sign of life around the house. "O'my gosh," Ben said, "you don't think he's already traveled on do you?"

"No, couldn't be," I said, "he wouldn't go without telling us."

Then from inside the house, "That you boys out there?"

"Yes sir."

"Well", as he opened the door, "com'on in and visit a spell on this fine sunshiny breezy Kansas day."

We stepped into what was the old kitchen area where he had his bedroll laid out. Along side was that little tin box. I sure wondered what was in that box, but figured I'd never know because I sure wasn't going to ask him. Ben held out the little bag with the hardboiled eggs and apple which Rusty took with a grateful hand, looked into the bag and said, "An apple a day will keep the scurvy away."

"Well sit boy's, sit."

Ben and I pulled up a place on the floor and sat. I noticed a half gone loaf of bread and an empty milk bottle on the floor so he'd obviously made the trek to Partridge for some food. From the strawberry tips in a little pile on the floor I figured he'd also made a short trip to our garden.

Rusty asked, "Any fish in that creek, boy's?"

Ben said, "Only when there's a whole lot of rain and the creeks off the Arkansas back up bringing fish with it—like now."

"What kinda fish?" he asked.

Ben said, "Mostly just catfish and carp."

Rusty said, "Now carp is a favorite food of the Chinese, but I'll tell you boy's, I ate so much carp the last time I was in China I don't care if I ever see or eat one of them low down bottom feeders again. But catfish, now that's one of the finest eatin' fish in the world; it's all in the fixin'."

I said, "Dad says they're both bottom feeding junk fish."

"Well boys," Rusty said, "as they say one man's junk can be another man's treasure. Take catfish for example, they're slippery devils but what you got'a do is peel that slimy black skin right off, slit it straight down the underbelly, and gut it. Head on or off, don't matter, right in that slit you stuff some cut-up tomatoes and onion and a little salt. If you got a frying' pan just fry it in deep lard maybe ten minutes and it's ready to eat. If you don't have a frying pan and you're working with a fire and spit out'a doors you take a green tree branch and stick it straight through that cat longwise and roast it for about ten minutes one side, turn it over and roast it ten on the other and boys I'll tell ya' you could be dining with the finest folks at Delmonicos in New York City. Where, by the way, I've eatin' many times."

I asked, "What's Delmocos?"

"Not Delmocos my boy, Delmonicos; one of the finest restaurants in the world. Why just a few months ago I lunched with Beau Jimmy Walker hiz-honor the mayor of New York City himself when he was looking for my thoughts on a problem he was having with the police department. Seems the policemen wanted to start carrying guns. They claimed with all the lawlessness a billy-club just wasn't enough of a peace-keeper anymore. What's this world coming to boys?—the lawlessness."

Ben asked, "What'd ya tell the mayor you thought he oughtta do?"

"Why I told the mayor I didn't see anything wrong with the police carrying guns just as long as there was no bullets in them guns."

"You know boys I once carried a gun—well a rifle actually—a U.S. Springfield. That's when I was in the Marine Corp during the Great War. When I graduated, class president, from Benjamin Harrison High it was either Harvard College on a scholarship or the military. I was lucky because in the first couple years of the war the draft age was 21, but by the time I graduated high school it had been lowered to 18. Well boys, I'd been wanting to get a crack at those Huns for a couple years and I wasn't about to pass up the chance when I had it. The heck with the scholarship, my further schoolin' could wait, so I up and joined the U.S. Marine Corps. My Mother cried, Dad said maybe they'd make a man out'a me, and away I went. That is, me and my pal Mo Mallory. Mo was from the deep South and had a real southern drawl, as in, ya'aalll. He was a stocky kid with coal black hair always in a short brush-cut that seemed like it never grow'd. Mo was our class crazy. You know how some people speak without talking? Just looking at 'em you know something's about to happen. Mo was where the action was. One time he accidentally shot another kid in our gang right in the head with a not hidden well enough pistol, but I won't get into that, the kid lived. Mo had a trick he liked to do; he'd hold his breath 'til his face got as red as a radish and his head looked as big as a melon and when you'd think he was surely going to explode he'd finally blow out his lungs like a shot out'a cannon.

He was just showin' off, but he sure got our attention. We went different ways in the Marine Corp, but I heard later that he was showin' off to some fellas and finally held his breath just a little too long and all the red blood vessels in his head burst, turning him into a half-wit, and he got throw'd out'a the Marines. That's the last I ever heard about Mo Mallory."

"Now boy's, let me tell you about me, the Marine Corp, and The Great War."

"After training camp I was assigned to the Second Division, got put on this old tub with a couple thousand other, soon to be seasick, guys and shipped over the Atlantic to LeHarve, France. We unloaded and were soon trucked onto Paris. All we saw of Paris was while marching through to the front. When the Americans first got into the war our allies complained that General 'Black Jack' Pershing was too slow in getting the American boys involved in the fighting, but by the time I was shipped over 'Black Jack' couldn't seem to get us to the front fast enough. Our destination was a place called Belleau Wood about fifty miles southwest of Paris that had been taken by the allies, then lost, and we were to try and take again. We weren't long out of Paris when the signs of war started showing up. Seems like for every one of us marching towards the front two weary, rag-tag troops, were marching towards the rear. These soldiers weren't in any kind of formation or nothing, just dragging their Springfields on slouched shoulders over the rain rutted dirt road, not saying nothing. Most looked like American doughboy's, but there were war-worn Frenchie's too, both with dirty bandages on heads, arms and legs and some struggling with make-shift crutches.

"After about five hours of marching west we could start to faintly hear the artillery fire—BOOM!, one thousand, two thousand, three thousand, four thousand, BOOM!—as the war was getting closer. We marched past some blown out stone and wood farm buildings with no signs of folks, a bloated cow or pig carcass now and again, and a few scrawny chickens scratching the ground for anything for their empty craws. Every now and then we'd pass a mutilated horse aside the road. They'd be military draft animals that wouldn't know nothing about taking cover in a shelling and they'd get their heads blowed off and belly's ripped open. These poor creatures weren't even candidates for a glue factory.

"By and by, our sergeant stopped us near a clump of trees and said that was where we'd bivouac the night, to get comfortable, and we'd be getting some hot chow soon. I'd take the hot chow but the getting comfortable wasn't probable. That evening a brass hat stopped by where my squad and others were still working at getting comfortable and having a smoke. He gave us an, "as you were," and the Captain, who looked like he just stepped from a recruiting poster, went on to remind us that we were Marines, we would likely do battle in the morning and for Marines retreat wasn't ever an option, and he gave us a parting, "good luck." With these reassuring words my buddies and I tried to find a soft spot on the ground to get some shut-eye. BOOM!, one thousand, two thousand, three thousand, four thousand, BOOM! Sleep wasn't an option either. I could see some men looking at what I assumed to be pictures of folks at home and more than one Marine had a tear trickling down his cheek. I got'a tell you boys I was scared and I knew the other fellas were too. There was sorta of a bond between us—we were all scared.

"We somehow made it through that first night to be called to attention in the morning and served up chow which was the last thing on my mind and I settled for coffee and a cigarette. My stomach had the skitters. I didn't see anyone else eatin' either, just everyone trying to look calm, but all betrayed by no denying fear in the eyes. This Belleau Wood that we were to take was just beyond a series of wheat fields, or what had been wheat fields, now clods of dirt and stubble, so we had to cross these open fields to re-take the Wood. About seven in the morning our sergeant blew a whistle for us to fall-in and get our marching orders. We got into a single straight line and started our march to soon move to a two abreast line. I was in the upfront line as we began to hear the signs of battle; rifle and machine gun fire, out front. We were at the edge of a wheat field now and got the whistle signal to move forward double-time. After we'd scampered about a hundred yards, well beyond the field perimeter, firing at will, men began to fall and the whistle came to hit the dirt which didn't come too soon for me. I rolled over on my back to relieve the pressure on my heaving chest and facing the heavens thought quickly enough to thank my new found Lord for getting me this far, but now if He really loved me He'd get me out'a there. Just for a flash I thought maybe I should'a taken that scholarship to Harvard College.

"We crawled on our bellies about another hundred yards or so seeming to me to just be getting into more serious trouble. There was enough barbed wire strewn on that battle field to enclose all the pastures in Kansas. We were an hour or so into battle and were pretty clearly pinned down. Our only break was for some reason we weren't takin' artillery fire. I could hear bullets splat, splat, in the dirt around me and the awful hollering and moaning as a near guy would get hit with zero prospect of medic help. Picture a clock boys; from our center the Germans had machine gun positions in hedges at 9, 12, and 3 o'clock. We were getting slaughtered and Marines don't retreat—not an option. Our communications had gone to hell, gone, poof! I think our whistle blower must have been hit or he swallowed his whistle. What in the hell were we to do? I was hugging the ground like I was married to it when I started thinking about the old USA and how I'd sure rather be there than here and it was home one way or the other. Now if I was going to make it home I had to get out of this very serious predicament and that was only going to happen if those machine guns were silenced. Those guns and those cursed Huns had to go—but how? Our command had vanished—shot or simply cowering in the field like most everybody else waiting for somebody to do something, or help to come. I tried communicating with the boys on either side of me, but all I got were empty, non-responsive blank looks. Then some guy jumps up firing at nothing and makes a run for the rear only to be cut down like a gobbler at a turkey shoot.

"If I could back out on my belly the way I came in without getting hit maybe I could flank the gun position at 9 o'clock and if I could get 9 o'clock maybe I could turn the gun on 12 o'clock and that could rally the troops to hit 3 o'clock. It was something. I had two grenades but couldn't use them to hit 9 o'clock without alerting 12 which would make it nigh on impossible to then hit it. I'd have to hit 9 with my rifle, bayonet, or both. How many men per nest? Two? Three?

"I couldn't just lay there waiting to get hit and without even thinking further found myself scooting backwards and then turning myself around I began moving out head first, belly scraping the rough ground, eluding entanglement in barbed wire. It was one of those times when I wished I wasn't so dang big. It was mighty slow goin' and I had about 200 yards or so to cover through the splat, splat, of bullets hitting the ground around me. Crawlin' along I got slapped in the face by a hand only to raise my head far enough to see I had been slapped by an arm dangling over a line of barbed wire but no body, no head, no torso, just an arm. I passed several boys laying flat out on the ground and a couple grabbed my wrist, eyes popping out from under their dish-pan helmets—"where are ya goin?—what'a you doin?" I said, "I'm getting out'a here that's what I'm doin'" They, "are you crazy—you'll get hit for sure—help'll get here." I said, "I aint waitin'!" I crawled around one dead Marine and closed his eyes as I went by. After about four hours, the wheat stubble having ripped through my khaki's, shredding my legs and belly bloody, I'd crept back to the edge of the wheat field where we had first entered this hell. Now I was in an area with some brush and trees and so some cover. I couldn't just get to my feet, but I could at least crawl on all fours and I started moving towards the area of the machine gun at 9 o'clock, about 150 yards away. I crawled on all fours 'til I was maybe 75 yards from the machine gun nest. The Krauts made it easy to find with their almost continuous firing. Now I had to go back to my bloody belly crawl to get close enough to see what I was up against. Following the, tac-tac-tac-tac, I soon spotted the barrel flash from the machine gun and the silhouette of two Hun's, one feeding, the other firing. I could get close enough to lob a grenade, but I couldn't tip off the machine gunners at 12 o'clock if I was to get a crack at them too. No, I had to rapidly pick them off, one, two, with my Springfield which shouldn't be to hard at 75 yards if I could just settle down and smooth my jitters. I still had to maneuver a shade as I was too much to their side and needed to be more at their back to get off clear shots so I crawled some more to that end. After about another half hour—it must have been about three o'clock in the afternoon by now—I was in as good a position as I was ever going to be in. The Hun's were totally occupied in blasting that infernal machine gun and I never once saw them look over their shoulder in my direction. I fixed bayonet just in case and assumed the shooting position—had a flashback of the firing range in basic—sighted the man doing the firing, squeezed the trigger, POP!, he fell, the other spun around and I squeezed again, POP!, he fell—got 'em both. I got to my feet and rushed the nest ready to fire again, or bayonet, if necessary, but they were both dead for sure. I turned them so I could see their faces and I swear one of 'em looked just like a copper that walked our neighborhood beat when I was a kid; the other just looked like a dead German with a big bloody hole in his face where an eye used to be. That would be number two who spun around when I hit number one. Now I had to put my head together to make my next move to try and knock out the 12 o'clock machine gun nest. One man feeding and firing a machine gun wasn't great, but it would have to be. Spotting the other nest was easy because they never seemed to stop firing. I looked out over the field and couldn't spot any of our boy's concealed in the wheat stubble, but did see the crumbled over bodies of those that tried to make a dash out only to be entangled dead in barbed wire. They simply couldn't move and stay alive. I pulled the Kraut bodies clear, took an ammunition box and propped it up to where I could lay a belt of bullets across the top of the box to feed the machine gun. That meant I'd have to fire in a burst, adjust feed, and burst again, but that was the best I could come up with. Nothin' complicated about the how-to with the machine gun. So now I honed in on 12 o'clock, looked to the heavens and again asked the Lord to be my mate, and let go a burst. Boy's I think I got one of those Hun's with that first burst. Their nest went silent for several seconds. Now I'm figuring I got one and the other is trying to figure out where the killer shots came from and what his next move should be. If I'm right he's got the same problem I had in trying to figure out how to feed and shoot at the same time. I gave him another burst. The 3 o'clock machine gun doesn't seem to be making any adjustments so I'm suspecting they haven't figured out what's happened. But, after my second burst 12 o'clock must have realized what had happened and he threw me a burst. By this time, realizing the firing pattern had changed, some brown helmeted heads began popping up on the field. I had the Hun at 12 o'clock busy and my guys now just had the 3 o'clock machine gun busy on them. And as long as my boy's kept their heads low I could cross fire a few bursts at 3 o'clock too, just to keep it off balance and stop that constant fire. So with number one out, number two crippled and number three erratic, the boys on the field were able to start to return fire.

The remaining German at the 12 o'clock nest I was firing on soon saw the turn in battle and waved a white cloth of some sort and came out of his nest with his arms raised. Our hundred or so boy's then rushed the remaining nest with rifle and grenades and quickly knocked it out—before the Kraut's waved any white flag. We took just the one prisoner. When it was over about 25 of our boy's lay dead on the field, but better than a hundred were still alive to re-group with battalion and move on and join the regiment in the re-capture of Belleau Wood for the final time.

It took about two more weeks of bloody fighting to re-take the Wood, but believe me boys when it was all over there were a lot more dead German's in that Wood than there were Americans.

"My buddies and our commander made a big fuss over me, but it didn't much effect where I slept or what I was fed. The Marines did make me a sergeant of a squad, with a little bit of a pay raise, and later on they had a ceremony where some general had his say and they hung a medal around my neck. I hav'ta say I was kinda proud, but heck the truth be known I was only trying to help get me and my buddies out'a one tough spot so we could maybe go home on our feet and not in a pine box. The war went on for another several month, but I didn't see a lot of action after Belleau Wood, which was all right with me; I'd seen enough suffering and death to do me a lifetime."

"So boy's, that was my life in the United States Marine Corp during the Great War—the war to end all wars."

I breathlessly said, "Boy Oh boy Rusty, you're lucky to be alive."

And Ben, "Yea, you're a real hero Rusty."

"Naw, I'm no hero, just did what I thought I had'a do. I saw plenty of hero's though lads; I surely did, and some of them ain't never comin' back."

"Holy cow Rick!" Ben said, We're late for lunch—let's get goin'."

"See ya later Rusty."

We ran home and arrived just as Mom stepped to the back porch with hands on hips and that—where have you been look on her face.

"Sorry Mom, we're here."

We got washed up and made it to the table just as Dad was pushing his chair away, "Remember you guys I want you two in the oats field this afternoon stacking those bundles into shocks so we can get in there with the hay wagon and clear that field tomorrow, OK?"

"Yea Dad," Ben said, "for sure."

Mom spread Ben and me out some lunch.

Dad, "Hey, where were you guys all morning?"

I said, "We were down at the 'little white house' visiting with Rusty and he was telling us about fighting the Germans in the war."

"O'yea, and I suppose he knocked off the entire German army single-handedly."

"No," I said, "not the entire Kraut army."

"Kraut, right, excuse me, Kraut army," Dad said, as the screen door closed behind him, "I'll be in the shop."

Ben and I finished our lunches, got our straw hats, work gloves, pitchforks, and headed for the field to shock the oats. That is, stacking the oats bundles in rows like a bunch of little teepees. That meant tomorrow morning Dad on the tractor pulling the hay wagon, we'd be in the field pitching oats, Mom probably pitching right along side. It took Ben and me the rest of the afternoon to get the oats bundles in their little teepee stacks and all the time we kept chattering about Rusty and his battle on that old wheat field in France. Was his story true? Why would he lie about something like that? It's true.

Since we knew we had our oats job in the morning, after supper Ben and I decided to trot down to the "little white house" to see what Rusty was up to, Mom saying as we went out the door, "One hour, no more" and Dad saying, "Ask

Sergeant York when he's leaving." It was dusk now and we could see a small fire flickering aside the house as we approached and when we got there Rusty was sitting by the fire twisting something on a stick over the yellow blue flame his head turned away from the smoke. "What's that?" I asked as we approached.

"It's a bull snake boys, tasty ol' bull snake."

Sure'nuff when I got closer I could see that it was a skinned snake with a long stick running lengthwise straight through its gutted body. It was browning like a sausage on a spit.

"You're just in time boys and I'd be happy to give you both a little morsel."

"No thanks," in unison.

Ben and I found our way to what had become our presumed log seats beside the fire.

Rusty said, "You boy's don't know what you're missing, why one time in the Belgian Congo me and the other survivors lived on snake meat for two months—snakes were bigger though—but that's a whole other story."

Survivors?—I sure wondered about that.

As I watched him eat the snake I couldn't help but wonder with that front tooth missing if he could still eat corn on the cob; maybe every other kernel. We exchanged "what'd you do today" and we apparently did more than he did as far as any form of work was concerned. He said he took a leisurely cool bath in the creek, trimmed his beard with his jack-knife and quite by accident caught a five foot bull snake which soon lost its head with same jack-knife, and finally he gathered a little fire wood. He was also, when he had a few moments, working on a plan to build a rabbit trap.

Rusty said, "I see a lot of cottontails running around here, but where are the jacks?"

Ben responded, "They like it out on the open field not in a grove. That's why the coyotes live at the edges of the fields where they can hide in the surrounding brush and lay in wait for a jack to hop by and then out sprint in the open."

Rusty said, "That reminds me of the Sarengetti and how

the lions stalk the wildebeest."

I asked, "The Sara Getty?"

"Yea, the Sarengetti."

"Hmm"

We could see that Rusty had slipped into our garden sometime or the other as he seemed to balance his diet with some fresh vegetables. I was thinking, he better not try and further balance his diet with a chicken or two or he'd have Dad to answer to. Rusty finished his snake on a stick and as he sat there on his designated log he picked up a stick and started poking the fire, "What'a you boy's gonna do when you're grow'd up?"

Both Ben and I said we really didn't know for sure, but Ben spoke up, "Since I'm oldest I'll probably farm the home place right here, kinda expected. Think I'd like that."

I said, "I think I'll go to college and then maybe move to the city like my uncles—maybe Wichita, maybe New York. Maybe I'll join the Marines."

Rusty said, "Well boys whatever it is you better plan on making yourselves some money. You know the Good Book says the love of money's the root of all evil, but if you don't love money just a little bit you'll get awful hungry—yes sir. Take me for instance I've had lots of regular jobs and some pretty good wages. Why just about a year ago I had a real good payin' job over in Ohio. We were building an aeroport in Columbus, to be named after my ol' war buddy Eddie Rickenbacker, and I was working for the dirt moving company on the blasting crew. We'd dynamite tree stumps and boulders and the like so they could smooth out the land. Well, my crew was working in an area that would be the end of an airstrip. There was a house nearby that had this big ol' mongrel dog that would come visit us every day and growl and bark at us—he just wouldn't shut up. We couldn't talk or think straight. It was really makin' us mad. Well, one of the guys in our crew, named Buck, had enough of this ol' dog and dreamed up a way to get the barkin' stopped. On this day the dog paid us his regular visit and charged at us a barkin' and a'growlin' and Buck very kind-like called for the dog with a sandwich from his lunchbox in his hand. Buck whispered something I couldn't hear to Charlie, the other guy in our crew. The dog stopped his barking and slowly came over to sweet talkin' Buck to see about the offering. Buck gave the dog the sandwich and at that instant threw his arms around the dog and then Charlie took hold the dog and Buck took some twine from his pocket and tied one end to the dogs tail. Then he took a stick of dynamite and tied it to the other end of the twine; about five feet of twine I guess. Then Buck took out a match, struck it, lit the dynamite fuse and yelled "LET'EM GO CHARLIE!" and that dog took off a'runnin', dragging that tumbling lit stick of dynamite, and where's he gonna run to? Home, of course. That dog high tailed it home and ran straight for safety under the house's back porch. He barely got under that porch and the dynamite blew—KA'BOOM! Well, that sure enough quieted that dog, but the blast also blew the porch and the back half the house to kingdom come. Fortunately the only one home was the dog. Well, to nobody's surprise the dynamite crew got fired, me included. So, I had'a move on."

Ben spoke up, "Boy, Rusty speaking of dogs we had one in Partridge last year they're still talking about. The benches in front of Joe Dillenbaugh's hardware store are a regular meeting place for some of the men around town. Dad calls 'em the village loafers making worldly decisions. The town dog, Jerry, a long haired black and white mongrel hung around them to get an occasional head scratch or belly rub. Roy, one of the regulars and the town prankster liked to play tricks on poor Jerry. For laughs he would sometimes grab Jerry by the tail, lift 'em and spin him a'round and round in a circle, fur flying, eyes popping, front legs straight out, then set him down and watch Jerry stagger, fall and stumble away. All the loafers had a good laugh. Well one day last summer Roy was spinning Jerry, lost his grip, and Jerry went flying into the front window of Joe's hardware store. Jerry survived—the window didn't. They say Jerry kinda stays clear of Roy these days and it's believed he's taken his last spin."

Rusty wasn't amused—"I'd like to spin that Roy a few times boys; that's what I'd like to do. Treat an animal like that."

"You know fellas I always get the travel itch; the wander lust, as they say. But I always pay my way. I noticed the grain elevator in Partridge has a sign posted looking for help during the wheat harvest, which would give me a few weeks wages—might just take that job. Point is boys, I can work a little and move on, work a little and move on. For me it works, but it aint for everyone, no sir, it aint for everyone. Gotta look at the down side; no fine sons like you boys, no wife to love, no regular home, no real friends, loneliness. That's the down side and I think on those things a lot. Then I get that foot itch and I wash those thoughts out'a my mind and move on. I don't have much, but I think you gotta say a persons freedom counts for something—doesn't it?"

"Speaking of money boys," as Rusty reached in his pocket and came out with a coin, "if you can come around tomorrow I'll tell you a little story about this here copper penny."

Ben said, "OK Rusty, but it'll have to be in the afternoon because Rick and I have a job gathering oats in the morning, but we'll be over tomorrow afternoon for sure."

Ben and I had to skedaddle quickly to get home by Mom's time line.

Lying in bed that night we couldn't get to sleep for thinking about what adventure Rusty might have for us tomorrow. Why it could be anything, from anywhere to anybody; tomorrow will tell.

We were up early, did our morning chores, and anticipating a serious work day had a big breakfast. Dad hooked up the hay wagon to the John Deere, threw on a couple pitchforks, made sure we had our shoes on, our straw hats and gloves and we chug-chugged to the oats field. Dad started down the oats rows with Ben and I walking alongside the wagon pitching the bundles from the oats shock onto the wagon. As we came around from the first field rotation Mom was waiting for us, pitchfork in hand, and she joined in on the oats pitching. She was as good a hand as the best of 'em and Ben and I were happy to see her—makes our job a little quicker getting done.

About one o'clock the field was clear of oats shocks, the wagon was loaded accordingly, and we headed for the barn. Dad had to go to town to the blacksmith shop to get some plow shears sharpened so pitching the oats from the wagon to the hay loft would wait 'til later. With Dad as the lead pitcher hay unloading wasn't the job loading was. Anyway, that would wait.

Mom fixed us some sandwiches and lemonade for lunch, and as she anticipated what our plans were, fixed a couple extra sandwiches for Rusty.

Dad said, "Let me guess—you guys are going over to the 'little white house' to visit the vagabond. Mother have you ever met this character?"

"No Daddy, but I just know from what the boys say he's no threat—you know he'll be movin' on soon—it's their nature—let 'em be."

Dad's response, "Yea, yea, yea."

Ben and I hurriedly took the path to the "little white house". It had started to sprinkle a little and as we got there we didn't see any sign of Rusty 'til he poked his head out the door and said, "In here boy's—think it's gonna rain."

We took the high step into the house; high because the original wooden steps were long gone. I handed Rusty the little sandwich sack which he peered into appreciatively with a "Thank your momma for me."

Rusty said, "Pull up a floor boys and sit down," as he doubled over his bedroll and cushioned himself down softly. "Now let's see boys, where was we," as he unclenched his fist exposing a copper penny. "O'yea, boys it's entirely possible that I took the very copper from the ground that's in this here penny and what's more I'm lucky to be alive to tell you the tale. You ask, "How's that? Well I'm a gonna tell ya."

"Not long after knocking out ol'Jack Dempsey I kinda got the foot itch, and anyway it was time I better make a little money to live on. Wouldn't you know scanning the newspaper I saw an ad that I swear was put in that there paper just for me. The ad said there were good high paying jobs, just for the asking, at a Kennicott copper mine in the Alaska Territory. Now boys, talk about adventure I'd for sure never been to Alaska. The ad said if you just show up at McCarthy, Alaska Territory, pass a physical, you were guaranteed a job. Now I'd have to get myself to McCarthy which was probably four thousand miles away. I went to the library and found myself an atlas so I could see where in tarnation McCarthy was and it showed I'd have to get cross country to Seattle, catch an ocean freighter up to Valdez, Alaska, then travel maybe a hundred miles inland to McCarthy. Could be done; I decided to do it.

"It took me eight days to thumb-it to Seattle, sometimes in an automobile and sometimes on the back of a truck. Once there I soon found the dock area and began asking questions about ships to Valdez. After a few days of scouting I was directed to a ship, the Tropicana, which was scheduled for Valdez in three days. I was referred to the 3rd mate who told me that if I'd work the boiler room as a fireman for passage they'd take me aboard. I said I would, and they did. A boiler fireman on a freighter working a eight hour shift was as back breaking a job as I'd ever had; a real killer. But for a four day ticket to Alaska and the probability of a big pay day at the copper mine at the other end, I stuck it out. When we got to Valdez I got off the Tropicana and sure didn't look back with any fondness. Now I had about a hundred miles to go to get back to the copper mine in the mountains and the town of McCarthy. I figured correctly that there had to be a train to and from the copper mine and the seaport. The train ran every other day and though it didn't have any passenger cars, and most of the cars were open gondolas, a guy could hitch a ride in a freight car. I arrived on an even day so could hitch a ride in just a matter of a few hours. So far, things were looking good. Though my back was sure aching from shoveling coal for four days I found the train that was getting serviced to make the return trip to the Kennicott mine. I'd been tipped off that the deal was for a couple dollars the train crew would look the other way when you hopped a freight car. I hopped a car and figured I'd wait to see if I was discovered before I coughed up a couple dollars; within twenty minutes out of Valdez I was a couple dollars poorer. I'd had enough sense when in Seattle to go to second hand store and get myself a heavy woolen hooded parka, a couple wool shirts, socks, some long johns and some heavy leather boots. Not long out'a Valdez in that freight car I undid my bedroll and had my blanket wrapped around me. It was November and though not one of Alaska's coldest winters it was a lot colder than I was used to, but I was OK. I left the car door open a crack and it wasn't long before I could see we were being swallowed by the biggest snow covered mountains I'd ever seen. Three hours out on a four hour trip the snow, which had been falling lightly, began to come down heavier and was drifting and banking in random configurations. I sensed the train laboring and slowing down to a crawl and then coming to a full stop. We sat there a bit and I decided I better try and get to the engineers cab to see what was goin' on and rather than fight the snow drifts I shimmied to the top of the rail car and trudged across the top and edge of the cars to the engineers cab. There were three men in the cab, now four, with the side curtains pulled down and the little door open to the coal fire in the engine belly. This being a new experience for me I naturally asked what, how, and when. They said we were stuck in the snow and wouldn't be going anywhere soon and maybe Kennicott would send along a rail plow or maybe we'd just be sitting there for several hours or more. They were warm, had packed lunches, a jug, and just didn't seem to be in any big hurry to get out'a there—this had happened before. I wasn't so prepared nor inclined to just sit and wait for help that may, or may not, be coming. The snow had let up considerably and I asked how far we were from McCarthy and they told me I could walk it in a couple hours, but that would be without the snow to contend with. They did say the snow had a tendency to drift intermittently and if I'd stay with the rail bed I would probably get good stretches between drifts where I could hike fairly easily and then work around the occasional drifts and snow banks. Something the train couldn't do. I think they kinda liked the idea of me going too thinking if I got to McCarthy the folks there would be alerted to the problem and work back with the snow plow and get the train movin' again. I decided to give it a go.

"I went back and got my bedroll and knapsack, all my worldly belongings, and trekked off around the first snowdrift that had stopped the train and as the fellas in the engine said it looked like I'd have fairly easy goin' as long as I stayed with the rail bed. I had to fight some pretty deep snow at times—up to my knees—but it drifted and banked a lot more off the rail bed than on because the road bed sorta perched above the grade around it and the wind kept the bed fairly clear. But then the snow, which had slackened, started to come heavy again; heavier snow and wind than before. The wind driven snow was now slapping at my face and stinging my eyes. After an hour or so I found myself fighting knee, then hip deep, snow. I wasn't sure I was still on the rail bed and frost and exhaustion were setting in. I thought I could still see an alley between the trees to my front which I thought must be the rail bed, but as the wind and snow kept whipping me I couldn't be sure. I was growing numb from the cold. I had to stop, see if I could find some shelter in the trees, and rest a spell; maybe wait out the worst of the storm. Over to my left side about fifty yards through the trees I could make out a rocky cliff behind a clump of trees; maybe some shelter from the snow and wind. I dug in and struggled through the snow in that direction and as I got to within about fifty feet of my goal there suddenly came a loud, spine chilling animal-like roar of a kind I'd never heard before. I quickly flattened out on the snow carpeted forest floor and just lay there for a few moments afraid to raise my head. Next I heard just a deep throated groveling sound like something was in real pain. Back in the trees towards the rocky bank I could see pretty good through the snow so I raised my head slowly and looked in the direction of the groaning. And then, not more than fifty feet away in front of me, was a image that will be with me 'til the day I die. There was a big fury old momma grizzly bear lying on her side trying her best to deliver a cub, but the cub wasn't coming. I raised to a squatting position to get a better look. The bear saw me and threw me a guttural roar and a swipe of a mighty paw, but she couldn't do much else. She kept groaning as I moved closer to see if I could better determine the state of delivery. She again swiped at me with a paw, but she was whipped. She normally would have been in a secure den somewhere doing this. Getting closer I could see that the cub was head first at least half way out. A lot smaller than I'd have thought. I carefully moved around to where I could grab the cubs tiny slippery front legs and pulled with all my might, which as you might see is considerable, but the cold and exhaustion had me weakened. Momma bear reared her massive head in my direction and I swear was looking at me square in the eye. I'm no mechanical engineer but I knew if I had any prayer of pulling that cub out I had to gain some leverage beyond my normal strength. I thought on it a bit and then I loosened my parka and took off my leather suspenders and belt; I don't know why I wore both, I just did. I took out my jack-knife and cut my suspenders into two sections that I tied together and then added and tied my belt to one end which gave me a leather strap about nine feet long. My parka hood had a heavy leather draw string that I pulled loose and then tied it around the cubs slimy front paws. Then I took my leather strap and tied it to the draw string giving me a nine foot leather strap tied to the cubs front legs. Now I had to find a downed tree limb, not too big around, and about six or seven feet long. In the spruce forest it didn't take long to find what I was looking for. All the time momma bear, moaning and groaning, was eyeing me through and through. The cold was brutal, but I had to push on. I took the found tree limb I needed and tied the leather strap to one end of the limb and the other strap end to the drawstring tied around the cub's paws. There were standing spruce trees all around us and I picked one, where it needed to be located for my plan, that was about five feet from the protruding cub. Then I took the pole and placed the pole lower center horizontally on the vertical backside of the standing tree. Picture a teeter-totter on its side with one end tied to the bear cub, the tree as the center pivot anchor, and me at the other end. Now I could pull or push on one end of the pole and get the leverage on the other end I hoped would pop the cub. I pulled on the end of the pole, raised a foot and pushed it against another tree for additional pressure; anchored my other boot heel in the ground, and grunted and pulled with all I could muster. Then I reversed positions and pushed mightily on the pole and suddenly POP/PLOP out slid the cub. Momma bear heaved, wheezed, and reared her head in the direction of the birthing. The cub was slimy with afterbirth, but looked to be alive. I retrieved my now somewhat sticky belt and hood draw string; the suspenders were finished. In spite of its ordeal the cub was soon on its legs and unsteadily found its way to momma's milk and began sucking. I think momma, who was totally spent, and me had a harder time in the birthing than the cub did.

"The trauma had caused me to temporarily forget how cold I was. We, that is me and my new friends, were kinda sheltered from the wind by being up against the rocky bank and the cluster of trees around us. I was exhausted and though staying there with that grizzly bear might mean death, I wasn't going anywhere—I couldn't. I took my blanket from my bedroll and very carefully, very slowly, crawled towards the hulking bear still sprawled prostrate on the ground. Her new-born, hunger satisfied, had nuzzled under the momma bears huge fury humpback shoulders. I had crawled close enough to the bear that I could put a hand out and touch her torso—it was warm and thick with fur. I eased closer and closer without getting any reaction from the bear, lay against her warm body, pulled my blanket over me and closed my eyes. With the bears heavy breathing reverberating against my backside, I quickly passed out from exhaustion.

"My next awareness, apparently several hours later, was when I was awoken and tumbled over as the hulking brown bear rose to her feet. I froze. Was I a dead man? Her big brown eyes glared at me and a glistening misty snort blew from her nose as she crooked her neck and delivered me a soulful bellow I thought not intended to terrorize. Her cub was at her feet as she turned away from me and in that bear lumbering gait, little cub wobbly in tow, began walking away, soon disappearing into the forest.

"The weather had let up, I was soon relocated on the rail bed, moved out towards McCarthy and was there in about an hours time. The townspeople were sure surprised to see someone trudging through the snow down Main Street as I looked for the rail office. I found it and told the guys there about the rail trip and about where the train was snowbound. They soon hooked up an engine driven snow plow and went for the stalled train.

"I didn't tell them about the grizzly bear—they would have thought me a madman.

"I asked about the Kennicott office which they directed me to and inside an hour I was hired to work at the mine tipple beginning the next day. They also directed me to a rooming house where I got a room, a hot bath to wash off the bear smell, and a warm meal.

"Obviously I was low seniority and the tipple job was heavy duty. To withstand the dust they equipped me with coveralls, dust mask, goggles and hood. I was reminded of that awful time I was lost in a sandstorm in the Sahara Desert. My boss was fair, I liked the fellas I worked with, and the pay probably my best ever. The little town of McCarthy was a typical mining town—saloons, gambling and naughty ladies—but, I pretty much kept to myself. I couldn't indulge in those sinful pleasures and besides I went there to make money, not spend it. I stayed about eighteen months, it was May, I'd saved good money and was ready to go south. I said good-bye to my friends at work and the boarding house, packed my sparse belongings, and headed for the train. The fellas at the train remembered me from the trip in and as thanks for helping them they invited me to ride back to Valdez in the engine cab, which I was happy to do. I got to Valdez, in picture perfect weather, made the same fireman deal on a ship as I did going up and soon sailed for Seattle. My Alaska adventure was over."

Ben spoke first, "WOW."
Then me, "HOLY COW."
Ben, "That's the greatest story I've ever heard."
Me, "Or ever will hear."
Rusty said, "Well boy's it was no walk in the park for sure, but it could'a been worse, the bear could'a et me. No boys, the fact is that each in our own way understood one another; momma bear got herself her life back and a healthy cub, and I didn't freeze to death. All three were winners."

I wanted to ask him about being lost in the desert in a sand storm, but it was getting to be time for afternoon chores, the milking, and supper, so we told Rusty we had to go but would be back sometime tomorrow depending on any plans Dad may have for us. As we headed home Rusty shouted after us, "you boys remember to thank your momma for the lunch."

Later at the dinner table Dad asked, "What'd you boys do this afternoon?—no let me guess—you visited with the travelin' man down at the 'little white house'—right?"
Ben said, "Yea Dad, he told us a real exciting story about going to Alaska."
Dad said, "Stop, let me guess, he wrestled with a grizzly bear and came out on top, now probably sports a bear skin cap and overcoat."
I spoke up, "Naw Dad, nothing like that; he actually made

friends with a grizzly bear."

Dad responded, "Mother, what's for dessert?"

Ben and I looked at each other with that, let's let it drop look and I said, "I'll have some dessert too."

The next morning Dad, Ben, Mom and me went to work clearing the seed-wheat acreage of renegade rye so the subsequent planting would be with pure wheat seed. Once in the field we'd line up about eight feet between us and then march through the field, like we were stirring up pheasants, and pluck the easy to spot rye which always stood about six inches higher than wheat. Back and forth 'til we covered the entire field. We started about eight in the morning and finished about one in the afternoon. Then it was head back to the house to wash up and have some lunch.

After lunch Ben and I headed for the "little white house" to see what Rusty was up to, but didn't find him around. We peeked in the door and saw his bedroll and that mysterious little tin box were still there so he was still in the area. We hung around for fifteen or so minutes but he didn't show. Maybe he walked to Partridge to get a job at the grain elevator, whatever, we knew he'd be back eventually, so we'd see him another time and headed home. Mom put us to work that afternoon weeding the garden and before you knew it chores, milking, supper, a game of whist, and bed.

The next morning we did our morning chores, helped with the milkin', had breakfast and headed down the path to the "little white house". As we approached the house we saw a little rising spiral of smoke though it seemed a little warm for a fire. As we got closer we could see Rusty sitting, his back to us, in front of the fire. So as not to startle him I shouted out, "Rusty," and he turned with that shy one tooth grin through his whiskers and said, "Morning boys—what a fine day we have." We were now up to him and quickly saw what the fire was all about. There was a skinned rabbit browning on a spit over the fire.

By golly, his trap worked.

"This here's gonna be my lunch lads—maybe I'll share a

bite with you if you'd like."

Ben, without much enthusiasm, "Maybe."

I out and out said, "No thanks." We just never much got into rabbit at home. Don't know why because in those times a lot of farm folks did eat rabbit. On the other hand jack rabbits, which were plentiful, weren't very good eating compared to the fewer cottontails. Whatever, we seldom indulged. We loaded up on chicken—loved fried chicken.

We didn't ask Rusty where he was the day before and he didn't say. Evidently it wasn't to get a job. He was slowly turning the spit, poking at the fire with a stick, and licking his whiskered lips. Rusty said, "I'm leaving you boy's my rabbit trap."

Ben reacted, "Great."

I spoke up, "You aren't leaving are you?"

"Not yet boys, but I am feeling rested and am beginning to think about where I'd like to be going next. Never been to California but I aint about to go there. You know boys they get serious earthquakes out there and the greatest scientists in the world say one of these days there's gonna be an earthquake so powerful that the whole state of California is going to break right off—float off into the Pacific Ocean—and just sink. No sir, I aint going there. Then down below there's Florida that snot-drop between the Gulf and Atlantic. Why those same scientists say if the ocean rises just one foot that whole darn state will be under water and I aint much of a swimmer—anymore. That's one thing you can say about Kansas boys—all you gotta worry about is being blowed away. No, I'm thinking maybe Montana, or Colorado. You know boys I've never broke a bronco—rode an elephant in India—but, never broke a bronco. Heck, it's a further fall off an elephant than a horse—yea, maybe Montana."

Rusty took the rabbit off the fire and holding one end of the stick-skewer he began picking at the roasted rabbit with his hand. "Hmm, hmm, boy is this good," as he swung the stick in our direction, but we both shook our heads, no thanks. The three of us were now sitting around the fire ring and I picked up a stick and poked and scattered the embers,

41

no need for a hot fire now. I sensed we weren't going to be seeing too much more of Rusty; he seemed to be getting that foot itch.

Rusty said, "Boys you probably think I'm kinda shiftless, only working when it suits me, movin' around having crazy adventures, no family, no responsibilities really. Well, I guess that's who I am. Could I live a different kinda life? Plant these here wandering feet of mine on a quarter section of land here in Kansas, raise a good family? Don't think sometimes I don't lay there on that bedroll at night thinking about such things. I don't know boys, I guess I am who I am. A fella can't always say I'm gonna do this or that, or be this or that. Sometimes what is, just is."

I couldn't believe it—he'd picked that entire rabbit off that stick, hit his chest with a fist, belched and said, "Boy was that good!" Then he picked up a twig, tore off a sliver, and began picking his teeth.

"You know, I like me boys and that's really important. You gotta like yourself to be happy. Believe it or not I always wanna do better. My Daddy always said—never be satisfied with what you got done today, always be thinking about what you can get done better tomorrow. I sure like you boy's and I think the future looks good for you both."

Rusty went on, "You boys run along now 'cause I tell ya eatin' that fat rabbit and doin' a few little chores of my own I need a little nap. You come back tomorrow and maybe I'll have another one of my adventures to tell you about; I can think of one already. It's a dandy."

We both said, "Bye Rusty, see you tomorrow; anything you need?" as we stood and turned for home.

"Not a thing boys, not a thing, see ya tomorrow."

Ben and I took the path home.

At dinner Dad asked why we were so quiet, but added that it was kinda nice for a change.

"Now Daddy," Mom said.

I guess Ben and I were both thinking about the same

thing—was Rusty ready to move on to his next adventure? Did he have the itchy feet? In bed that night I thought about what he had said—never be satisfied with what you got done today, always be thinking about what you can get done better tomorrow—as I drifted off to sleep.

The next morning at breakfast Mom was saying "slow down, slow down, what's the big hurry?" as we rushed through breakfast and then hurried through our morning chores. Chores done, Ben and I took the path to the "little white house" at a fast, but apprehensive pace. There was no sign of Rusty outside the house, nothing roasting over a fire. Ben shouted, "Rusty, Rusty," with no response from out or in the house. We moved towards the house door, Ben reached up for the knob, turned and opened the door and took that big step up with me close behind. "No Rusty," Ben said, "he's really gone."

The bedroll, the tin box, the wall pictures were all gone. The rabbit trap sat in the middle of the floor and there was a note along side. Ben picked up the note and read: Boys it was a pleasure. Tell your Momma and Daddy thanks. As I move on I leave you with this old Irish blessing—probably stolen from a Scot—

> May the Road rise to meet you. May the
> wind be always at your back. May the Sun
> shine warm upon your face. May the Rain
> fall softly upon your fields and may God hold
> you in the hollow of His Hand.

And another thing…

Ben and I, both unable to speak, backed to the wall and slowly slid our behinds to the floor and sat there dumb-struck.

After a bit, "What did Rusty mean—and another thing—" Ben wondered.

We both knew it was coming, but were nonetheless

unprepared to see Rusty move on.

I said, "Do you think we'll ever see him again?"

Ben said, "I don't think so—maybe he'll write."

"Do you really think so Ben? Maybe he'll write about some adventure."

Ben said, "yea, maybe—we better get along home, nothing here no more."

But then Ben said, "Wait a minute—let's see what's up in that attic."

Alarmed I said, "NO WAY, NO WAY."

"Aw, com'on, you knew one day we'd hav'ta look— Rusty would."

With reluctance, I said, "How we gonna get up there?"

A pause, then Ben said, "We'll carry in one of the logs from the fire ring, prop it against the wall, you can give me a boost and standing on top the log I think I can reach the trap door. What'a you say?"

"All right, all right, but let's hurry."

We went outside and with considerable effort managed to maneuver a fire ring log into the house and propped it against the wall below the trap door. Now ready, I cupped my hands and Ben grabbed me around the neck, slipped a foot into my clasped hands and boosted himself to a standing position. Then he put a foot on one shoulder and boosted first one foot, then the other quickly to my other shoulder, and then a step to the top of the upright log. It was a good thing it was quickly because my shoulders were about to collapse.

I said, "You sure you wanna do this?"

Ben responded, "We hav'ta."

"Then hurry."

Ben eased up the trap door, slid it aside, and slowly, hesitantly, poked his head into the black hole.

"What'a you see? what'a you see?"

"It's kinda dark, but absolutely nothing. Wait a minute, here's a fold of paper—I'm climbin' down."

Ben made it to the floor, certainly bruising my shoulders, though not falling, and quickly opened the note and read it.

"Well?" I asked.

Ben looked at me, smiled, and said "It says, 'make life an adventure'. That's Rusty's, 'and another thing'."

I picked up the rabbit trap, even if never used again, just to show Dad what Rusty could do. We headed home and went right to Mom to tell her about Rusty leaving and the notes he left anticipating getting a sympathetic ear, but she said, "There shouldn't be any surprise here—you knew from the first day you met him that he'd soon be traveling on—that's who he is. Wasn't he from here there and everywhere? Now his there is somewhere else. Remember this boys, while you're sitting here all sad he's gone, he's happy as he can be to be on the move again. You know what though,? I think he's going to miss you both."

Ben said, "Do you really think so Mom?"

"Sure do," Mom said, "and you know what else, another day or two and your father probably would have told him to move on anyway."

That proved to be good insight, because at dinner that evening Dad said, "I think it's time the prince of vagabonds moved on, maybe to that job at the elevator in town, or maybe to Niagara Falls so he can go over the falls in a barrel and live to tell you about all the things he did on the way down."

"Now Daddy," Mom said.

I spoke up, "Rusty's gone Dad. We guess he left sometime during the night. Ben and I went over to the "little white house" this morning and he was gone. Only thing left behind was the rabbit trap he made and a little note for Ben and me."

Dad said, "The what! the rabbit trap, you've got to show me this. If he can build 'em why doesn't he sell 'em? Maybe we can sell it and get the money to cover the vegetables he borrowed from the garden."

"Now Daddy," Mom said.

Dad said, "Oh all right, so he's here and gone, no real harm done, now let's talk about some jobs waiting to be done around here."

So, there it was, seven summer days gone by, but not likely to fade from memory any time soon. After that Ben and I often talked about Rusty's past adventures and in our minds concocted possible new adventures. Oh, there was no question that he was out there somewhere doing something exciting, maybe dangerous, or maybe noble; no question about it.

END

EPILOGUE

It was several months later, on a Sunday after church and dinner. Dad was sitting in his easy-chair reading the Hutchinson Herald, Mom was cleaning up the dishes and Ben and I were sitting on the floor playing checkers.

Suddenly Dad let out a gasp, said "Mother get in here and listen to this!"

Mom hurried in, "What for goodness sakes?"

Dad said, "I'll tell you what, let me read you a little item from page two of the Herald."

Mystery of Body in Barn
Turns Interesting

Garden City, Kansas: Max Brown a farmer residing four miles north of Garden City reported on Thursday past he discovered the body of a man in his barn loft. It appeared the man had bedded there for several days or longer. Mr. Brown called in the Finney County Sheriff who surmised that the body laying on the bed roll appeared to have experienced a natural death. The body was removed to the coroner's office and the subsequent inspection of the death site grew intriguing. The investigation, in addition to the bed-roll, turned up a knap-sack containing a few items of clothing, a jack-knife, a couple pictures, a worn book of poem's, *LEAVES OF GRASS*, by Walt Whitman, and a bar of soap. Also found was a small flour tin and in the tin were forty-three dollars and change, a Sinclair Oil Company map of Montana, an envelope containing what appeared to be an adult front tooth, and a small blue felt covered hinged box. The box held a metallic star centered medal connected to a blue neck ribbon. Under the medal was a faded, folded, piece of paper that read:

This Medal Of Honor presented to Sergeant William Wallace for gallantry in action when with little regard for his own personal safety he took heroic action resulting in the saving of as many as one hundred or more of his fellow Marines. Sergeant Wallace single-handedly eliminated one enemy machine gun position, dismantled a second facilitating the elimination of a third. This brave action was decisive in the American and her Allies subsequent re-capture of Belleau Wood, a critical Allied objective, 10 June, 1918.

> From a Grateful Nation
> Respectfully
> Woodrow Wilson
> President of the United State
> 1 October 1918

The sheriff's office checked the War Department for verification of the facts and to determine if there were any surviving relatives to advise of the death. The facts bore out and there were no known relatives.

It was found Wallace was born in New Castle Pennsylvania, November 4, 1900 to the Reverned Walter Wallace a Presbyterian minister and Dorothy Baxter Wallace a grade school teacher. There were no siblings.

The Pleasant Plains Cemetery is donating a burial plot and the Garden City American Legion Post #186 committed to raising the necessary funds for an appropriate head stone *and a proper military burial.*

Dad finished reading us the story and said, "Garden City, wonder what he was doing out there?"

Ben spoke up, "He was working his way west to the ranches in Montana."

"Yea," I said, "he'd never broke broncos before."

Dad sat back in his chair, put the paper on his lap, sighed, "Montana, working his way west, I'd just bet he was."

The Great Indian Raid of 1910

The Grants lived on a farm in South Central Kansas in the year of our Lord 1910. They grew wheat, oats and alfalfa, though Joseph Grant had also become a mule trader; probably the most successful mule trader in Reno County. He was what might be called a gentleman farmer. He may have worn denim bib overalls, but his shirts were starched, and when he was mule trading he always wore a fedora. His nails may have been soiled by day, but they sparkled by night. The Grant farm was a grade or two above the typical; a two story white frame house with a sweeping front porch and mansard roof—the handsome home of a successful man. The barn and other outbuildings were also painted white, like a Kansas cloud. Mr. Grant and his wife Clara, who also carried herself with extraordinary dignity, had one son, named Gilbert, or Gib. Gib, eighteen at the time of our story, was not an ordinary kind of lad. He was about six feet tall, stout, good-looking, with dark brown hair, green eyes, and had the reputation in the farm community as being quite a hellion. A reputation, to the chagrin of his parents, he seemed to enjoy. Gib really didn't search for mischief, it just seemed to unavoidably seek him out. From the time a small boy when he planted the bull snake in his teachers lunch pail, to when as a teenager he smuggled and released three baby skunks right in the middle of Preacher Richards sermon; he defined mischievous. The local matrons were certainly willing to overlook his rogue manner when perusing for prospective mates for their eager milk-maidens. He was a solid farm hand, his mom and dad were quite proud of him irrespective of his devilish ways, and the farm and the mule trading business would be his one day.

The Grant's 320 acre half section farm was just a couple miles south of the town of Partridge, population 250. One might assume that Partridge was named after the bird, as, *in a pear tree,* but it was actually named after a bird of another feather—an executive with the Santa Fe Railroad who, truth be known, had never set foot in Partridge, or in all probability, the state of Kansas. The Santa Fe line ran the north end of town and the Rock Island line the south end with about a quarter mile of dirt Main Street running between.

About mid-Main sat the gray cinder block Nixon's Drugs and out front on either side of the door were two wooden benches; quite old benches as evidenced by the smooth aged buttocks indents. These benches hosted the daily meetings for the towns "bench warmers" club. The only expectations for membership in the club were a willingness to consider and opine as to the local to worldly issues of the day, be in no hurry to get anywhere, and maybe do a little spitting and, or, whittling.

Joseph Grant on occasion would hitch a couple mules to a wagon, and a handsome wagon it was, and send Gib to town for an errand or two; a stop at the lumber yard, drop off some plowshares at the blacksmith shop for sharpening, pick up the mail at the post office, and the like. Sometimes Gib would stretch his town visits a bit, stop at Nixon's drug store for a pop, and catch the current news from the boys on the bench.

Gib made such a detour one day in July of 1910; a day that birthed an incident that would live in infamy for the town of Partridge.

The club members were jawing about the local, state, national, and international news when, for who knows why, they got to talking about the outlaw Dalton brothers from down around Coffeyville. The Partridge State Bank sat right across the street from Nixon's and two of the old timers said that years ago Bob and Grat Dalton robbed that bank in broad daylight and made off with over two-thousand dollars.

Another said, "They did stop by the bank all right, but it was to put money in not take it out."

But yet another, "The Partridge Bank didn't even exist at the time of the Dalton brothers bank robbin' days."

Somewhere therein, lies the truth.

Then the men made a natural transition from cowboys to Indians; redskins, and their place in Kansas folk lore. Central

Kansas was once inhabited by Indians of the Kansa, or Kaw, Tribes. The Kansas were high spirited planters and buffalo hunters who inhabited the territory for a few hundred years until rapidly pushed aside by waves of new settlers right after the Civil War. People in these parts were still somewhat wary of the redskins surmising they probably weren't to happy about being forced off their land.

The bench warmers dialogue went something like:

"The Kansas were supposed to go down to a reservation in Oklahoma, but some didn't go and thems that did didn't all stay, some came back."

and

"When my grandparents homesteaded here they had to regularly fend off the Kansa savages from raiding their farm for horses, cattle, or whatever else the red devils could steal."
"I don't know, I've been around here for thirty plus years and I think I've seen two, maybe three Indians—they all been run off long time ago."

and

"I've heard that Johnson woman that disappeared right out'a her home over there north of town five years ago was abducted by Indians and never has been seen or heard from since."
"Hogwash! if the Indians were going to abduct somebody it wouldn't have been that old hag."

and

"Anybody believes there's no Indians in Reno County gonna believe there ain't no sunflowers in Kansas either."

Gib was enthralled by all this talk about Indians. He'd

never seen one, that he knew of anyway, although his dad said in the past he'd done some trading with 'em and never had any problems. He remembered from his high school class on Kansas history that the Kansas lived in Central Kansas, in cone-shaped lodges, and he couldn't forget that the men plucked all the hair out'a their heads except for a lock they left running down their backside. That's about all he remembered about the Kansas.

As the men moved from Indians to international issues Gib figured along about then his dad would be looking for him, and he'd heard about enough for one day anyway, and as he turned the wagon for home he got to thinking and visualizing what would happen if a band of Indians did come a'gallopin', hoopin' and hollerin', up Partridge's Main Street. Why it'd scare people silly; that's what Indians do to people.

At home that evening, in deep contemplation, he couldn't get the subject off his mind—a band of savages raiding Partridge, Kansas. Why it'd be the biggest thing to hit Reno county in all its history.

At dinner that evening his mother asked, "Where are you anyway? You haven't heard a word we've said all supper."

"I'm here Mom—just tired—think I'll turn in early."

He'd sleep on it; maybe dream on it.

By the roosters am crow Gib had reached a momentous decision—he alone, through his tremendous ingenuity and imagination, would orchestrate an Indian raid on the placid village of Partridge. A raid the community would not soon forget.

To pull off the raid he had to gather the necessary paraphernalia to simulate an Indian war party, and accomplishing all without his mother and father the wiser. Wouldn't be easy, but he could do it. Where there's a will, there's a way.

He had saddle-broken one of the field mules, old Oscar,

but he wasn't going to attempt to do this thing riding Indian style bareback, he'd just drape a saddle blanket over the saddle and when nearly dark no one would be the wiser. To pass off Oscar the mule as an Indian pinto pony he'd apply a few splatterings of barn whitewash on its belly and rump and run a white lightning strike down a rear flank and leg. He'd obviously forego the Kansa custom of going bald, except for a lock hanging down the back, and would settle on a bandana anchoring a couple chicken hawk feathers he pulled from that hawk he'd shot a few days ago. The Indians brewed their body paints from roots and berries, but for his war paint he'd settle for some of that whitewash and some of his mothers blue denim dye. He'd have to forego a breech cloth and settle for some sawed off longjohns; he'd go barefoot. He'd have to create some real racket if he was to be taken for a band of Indians and for that he'd rope-tie and drag four or five old milk pails. In the likely event he may start a small fire or two he'd carry a canvas water bag filled with lamp oil. The time of day to pull off his raid was critical. It couldn't be full daylight where his ruse would be exposed, but not so dark that he'd just blend into the night. Probably the best time would be about 7PM; sorta at late dusk.

He gathered and stored his props in the barn behind a few bales of hay. The appointed evening he'd tell his folks a bit of a fib about going to visit a neighboring farmer friend for a spell. His plan was completed and he was confident, perfected.

The day of the planned event went very slowly for Gib. He was working in the field and repeatedly glanced at the sun to track the time of day. Finally the sun indicated it was time to call it a day and go in and wash up for supper, during which his mother said, "Gib, what's your hurry—you're swallowing your food whole."

His dad interjected, "He's just put in a hard days work mother—he's re-fueling—let 'em be."

Finishing supper he asked his mother if he could eat his dessert later as he was anxious to get going. She agreed,

"Don't be too late now."

Quickly he was to the barn. He pushed aside the hay bales to get at his props and stripped to his cut off long-johns, he'd go bare foot, bare chest, tied a bandana around his head and stuck in the three hawk feathers. He painted some stripes on his face and chest with the white wash and the blue dye. His prey wouldn't be able to distinguish the blue war paint in the near-dark, but he'd know it was there, warrior-like. Then he carried the bucket of white wash to Oscar's stall and painted some white blotches on his gray torso and a lightning strike down a rear flank and leg. Oscar didn't stir as apparently even the old mule knew to expect the unexpected from Gib. Gib then saddled up and draped a horse blanket over the saddle. He had his canvas water bag filled with lamp oil draped over the saddle pommel, some stick matches. He had pre-tied together four old milk buckets and wrapped a muffling horse blanket around them to avoid premature clanging. He went through a mental check-list; he was ready to go, took a peek towards the house to make sure all was quiet, mounted Oscar and slipped out the backside of the barn and turned Oscar towards Partridge at a trot, not a gallop, easy does it. His timing looked good thus far. He hadn't noticed 'til they were about a mile from home that Shep had tagged along. No matter, he was just an old gray and black hound and if he wanted to tag along, why not; besides he'd make a little noise too.

He arrived at Partridge just at the daylight condition he had hoped for, getting dark, but not quite there yet. His plan was to do an N through town. He'd start off at the south end of Main Street, which was on the westerly side of town, gallop north to the end of Main, then cut a diagonal back southeast right though the village residential center, to the southeast corner, and then turn to the north again up to the end of Ash, and then, raid completed, turn and hightail it for home.

He was at the south end of Main at the Rock Island tracks. One bit of fortuitous luck he wasn't counting on—at the railroad depot and Main was a livestock pen holding maybe thirty hogs waiting to be transported to market. How appropriate to orchestrate a hog stampede right up Main Street. Splendid!

It was now near dark and he rode Oscar over to the hog pen, leaned down and flipped the gate latch, slowly guided Oscar to the back of the pen, unraveled his old milk buckets from their wrap and lowered the buckets to the ground. He whispered, "Oscar, Shep, are you ready?" and at that moment he dropped the buckets, heeled Oscar in the hindquarters and screamed, "YIPEE!, YIPEE, YI, O!—YIP, YIP!, and AWAY!" The hogs squealed and bolted through the gate dashing straight up Main, grunting, snorting, and squealing, like they were being chased by a butcher. The clanging buckets, along with the crazed Indian yelling, creating a deafening ruckus. Shep joined into the mayhem by barking, WOOF! WOOF! WOOF! and nipping at the hogs heels.

Lamps started going on in the houses on Main as Gib and his band of bloodthirsty marauders ripped up Main. "CLANG! CLANG! CLANG! Gib began hearing shouts of "INDIANS! INDIANS!" In a matter of minutes the rampaging entourage was at the north end of Main, the hogs had scattered to who knows where, Gib turned Oscar to begin the diagonal gallop right through the neighborhoods heading to the southeast side of town. As they made the turn he slowed Oscar momentarily so he could get a handle on his canvas bag of lamp oil, and immediately came upon his first outhouse, which he doused with a splash of lamp oil, lit and tossed a stick match, and flames quickly engulfed the lonely privy. He resumed his gallop dragging the infernal clanging milk buckets CLANG! CLANG! CLANG! Shep yipping, all the time—Gib shouting the most authentic Indian yell imaginable, "YA WHO! YA WHO! YIPEE! YIPUM!" More house lamps were going on and he could see some discombobulated people scurrying here and there, running for their very lives, "INDIANS! INDIANS!" and he reciprocated with "KAW! KAW! KAW!" He thought he heard a shotgun blast or two, but neither he, nor Oscar, nor

Shep were hit. At random he torched three more outhouses as he galloped to the southeast corner of town. No more than ten minutes had passed since the raid began. Now he turned north for the final leg of spreading devastation and terror. "YIPEE! YIPEE! YI'O!" More house lamps went on, people dashing to and fro, looking for refuge from the unprovoked Indian attack.

CLANG! CLANG! CLANG! He torched one more outhouse. He was going to pass that one, but it was a two, no, three-seater, which he just couldn't pass—who do they think they are? "KAW! KAW! KAW!" He reached the culminating north end of town, and as loudly as he entered town, as quietly, he exited. The entire raid couldn't have lasted more than twelve, maybe fifteen, harrowing minutes. Gib looked back towards town and could see the intermittent flaming privies and folks running around willy-nilly with lanterns undoubtedly trying to discover how many town-folks had been massacred. Grinning, he turned the spent Oscar towards home, and with Shep running along side, was there in about twenty minutes. He and Oscar slipped into the barn and began regrouping. He got a bucket of water from the stock tank and washed the whitewash off Oscar and the war paint off himself; got back into his overalls, shirt and shoes, put the battered milk buckets back on their rack, the canvas bag wouldn't again be fit for water, gave Oscar an extra ration of oats and an affectionate pat on the head, then he and Shep walked back up to and in the house. Shep went straight to his usual spot at the feet of Mr. Grant—"Why on earth is Shep panting so?"

Gib said, "I'll have my dessert now Mom."

The aftermath:

As told later the town of Partridge lay in near ruin following the bloody raid by "twenty to thirty savage Indians."

The Acme Packing Company offered a $500 reward for

the arrest of the perpetrating Indians and made a demand for restitution for the loss of three hogs, never recovered, and the estimated loss of approximately 300 pounds of weight off the hoof due to the hogs being stampeded.

"That horse looked to me like it had the ears of a mule"
"Are you crazy, when's the last time you saw a spotted pinto MULE?"

The Kykendahl kids had a Shetland pony tethered in their side yard apparently frightened to death by the marauding Indians. "Why the pony's mane stood straight up, its bristly tail straight out, and its eyes near popped their sockets."

Mendoza the Mexican who worked the Santa Fe section gang loaded himself, wife and two tots on a railroad handcar and was last seen pumping his way west outta town.

They say the next morning there were ten treed cats that refused to de-tree; the last of which was finally coaxed down a week later.

The volunteer firemen responded to the call "FIRE! FIRE!" but pushed the pumper back in the shed when they found that it was only random outhouses that were blazing.

They say Ray Crotts was in his outhouse at the time of the conflagration, but escaped in a stutter step with his pants down around his ankles, arms flailing, and cursing at a sinful level.

Long time Partridge resident, the 98-year-old widow Jones, expired that night, but there's no conclusive evidence the savage's rampage contributed to her passing.

"Did you see the fangs on that wolf?"
"Looked a lot like the Grant dog to me."

It was confirmed that as a result of the stampede an opossum was flattened on the earthen Main right in front of the Nixon's drug store. Forever after, whenever a stranger visited the bench warmers, and heard the tales about the raid, one of the regulars would point to the street—"That's the spot, right thar—splat!"

The Hutchinson Herald sent a reporter down to do a story with the theme—does the Indian raid foretell a resurgent Indian uprising?

The Reno County Sheriff made an investigation and surmised—"We feel this was just the malicious act of a few disgruntled young Indian bucks and see no reason for panic."

So, that was the great Indian raid on Partridge, Kansas, June 29, 1910. No conclusive deaths, unless you count the Kykendahl's Shetland pony, no scalps lost, little property damage, and a couple hundred people lived to tell the tale, to tell the tale, to tell the tale....

And, as for Gib Grant? "I don't know what you're talking about."

END

EPILOGUE

Gib married Pansy Watson in 1915, had a daughter Peggy in 1917, was farming exclusively as the mule trading gave way to the tractor, and died in 1920. He was a victim of the great influenza epidemic of that era. The Partridge community mourned the loss, but he departed leaving lasting memories.

Skippy's Short Summer

It's been about sixty years ago now. Though ungodly early from other than the rooster's perspective, down in the barn Uncle Leon had already finished the milking. My three older brothers, younger sister and I were either stirring-in or rolling-out of bed. We slept on bunk beds in one large screened-in room that ran the back thirty-five foot width of the house. Mom, a pretty fortyish woman of medium frame and black, gray-flecked hair, was in the kitchen fixing some breakfast as evidenced by the sound of pan clanging and the aroma of frying bacon. "Rise and shine you guys. Can't sleep the day away. Things to do you know."

The farm had been in my mothers' Graham family since homesteaded in the late 1800s.Under the Homestead Act of 1862, a homesteader had to be at least twenty-one years old and household head to claim 160 acres of land—a quarter section. The homesteader had to live on the land, build a home (at least 12 by 14 feet), and farm for five years to claim clear title. The original filing fee was eighteen dollars and the final fee six dollars. The Grahams qualified.

This was primarily wheat country and standing center field in season and turning 360-degrees, a blanket of waving yellow wheat was about all the eye could see; the only variables on the horizon an intermittent grain silo or windmill reaching skyward yet dwarfed by the infinite amber-carpeted, blue-domed, prairie.

Dad was raised on the neighboring Andrews' farm, also homesteaded, and Mom and Dad attended the same one room, multi-grade, twenty-two pupil, school house within what in those days was an acceptable walking distance, about three miles for both Mom and Dad. Mom always said there was no way they were childhood sweethearts. She said she really didn't care for him much, in fact didn't care for him at all. Nonetheless, they ultimately moved from the little school house to graduating college, and Dad law school. Dad did his time as a doughboy in WW I France, while Mom taught school in a little Kansas town. They eventually re-discovered one another; or was it discovered one another? Mom's opinion of Dad apparently having changed, they married, and found their way to domesticity in St. Louis. But, as is said, "you can take the boy (or I suppose the girl) out of the country but…"and when I was about seven years old, with farmer neighbors as labor crew, our family built a little white clapboard summer house on my mother's old home place which was now lived on and farmed by her older brother Leon.

Uncle Leon cut a Rockwellian figure of a farmer—pale forehead, brown weathered lower face, gray mustache, stocky build, denim bib overalls and work-beaten dusty straw hat, all atop worn leather clodhoppers. When in deep concentration, as in turning a wrench in the belly of the old John Deere, he had the habit, and dexterity, to fix the tip of his tongue to the tip of his nose. Not sure that's necessarily a good thing, but he could do it.

He had a trophy wall in the shop. Rats would foolishly on occasion raid the granary only to be stalked and shot dead by Uncle Leon with his trusty, rusty, .22. He'd chop off the invader's tail and nail it to the shop wall. My last count was eighteen rat tails.

Then there was the infamous "pugh from the pew" incident. Seems Uncle Leon somehow had occasion to tangle with a skunk while in his Sunday shoes. The next church-going Sunday in town at First Pres, Uncle Leon and Aunt Emma were among a cluster of folks in mid-church at the beginning of service, but—by the benediction, they were the sole folk at the center of an otherwise void ten foot circle.

Uncle Leon was a kind and good man. That being said, the disappearance of Oscar the goat, to this day, remains a mystery.

Every summer the day after school let out, we loaded up and Dad drove Mom and five kids 500 miles west from St. Louis via US 40 & 50 to the family farm in South Central Kansas and back again in September. (During WW II this meant 35 mph and an overnight at the U-SMILE MOTEL just on the east side of Kansas City). Mom, Dad, and five kids in a 1940 Plymouth two-door sedan; no air condition-ing, of course. All the new, for-the-trip, comic books had been read by forty miles west of St. Louis. I think we kids got along reasonably well, however, that was when we first learned that Dad could handle the car nicely with his left hand and still be able to reach back and whack somebody in the backseat with his right. Somehow, by the apparent grace of a travel god, in time we would make it west to the Kansas farm. After safely depositing us on the farm Dad, after a few days, would return to St. Louis to provide for our living, but over the summer he'd manage a couple trips west to see how we were getting on.

Anyway, after breakfast of bacon and farm fresh eggs, which as far I could tell always tasted a lot like store bought eggs, I slipped into my uniform of the day, and every other day, blue denim bib overalls unencumbered by underwear, shirt, shoes or socks. I trekked the hundred or so paces over the dirt path to our cousins' house.

There were inherent hazards in going barefoot; stickers in the farmyard and cow pies in the barn yard. Stickers come in two varieties, one about the size of a pea with around ten prickles, and the easier to spot marble size with around thirty prickles. They both hurt like the dickens when pricking the soft underbelly of a youthful bare foot. Cow pies come in two varieties; squishy or crispy.

Upon arrival and morning greetings the collective group started the "whata' ya' wanna' do's?" There were also five kids in their family so we had an on site play pool of ten kids, six boys, four girls. Their family included identical twin girls—Mary and Maggie. They were easily distinguishable though because Maggie had a little brown mole on her cheek and one eye that was indecisive as to the direction it wanted to take. One of her brothers had a peculiar speech problem. Little Daniel couldn't say "yes." He could say "yellow," "you," "yonder," and so on. Just not "yes." In lieu of yes he would say "Wah." So it would go—"Daniel sing *Jesus Loves Me* for us." And we would get, melodically pleasing enough, "Wah, Jesus Loves Me—Wah Jesus Loves Me—Wah Jesus Loves Me—The Bible tells me so...." Jesus must have loved him all right, because by the time he was seven he got over the "Wahs."

The play options were plentiful. We had a cowboy saloon that originally was a truck bed travel trailer. Hanging from a huge cottonwood tree we had what was thought to be the tire swing with the widest arc in the county. The pivotal tree had a dual trunk. The primary trunk went straight up and a high limb anchored the swing rope. The secondary trunk rose at an easy to climb up slope and was our path to two cast-off points, high and higher. It couldn't have been designed better. It's as if God thought, "I've got an idea." A leap from cast-off point number two and you would surge precariously skyward as an exhilarating thrill-chill trickled down your spine. Uncle Leon at auction acquired all the playground equipment from the old abandoned one room school he and his siblings attended as children. Included were a merry-go-round, sliding board, teeter-totter, and swings. We weren't hurting for things to do, it was just where to begin. He also acquired the big cast-iron school bell that became the calling bell for the cows to come in for the evening milking.

As cousin Roy was saying, "How about cowboys, but this time I be a good guy?" we were startled by movement in the weeds and the subsequent appearance of a little gray, black-blotched, pup. "Looks like a wire haired terrier." The pup moved directly to the center of the kid cluster and with his stubby tail twitching began to play licky-face. No barking, just that "boy am I glad to see you guys" dog murmur.

"Where'd he come from?" said cousin Maggie. "I know all the neighbors dogs and I aint never seen him before."

"Besides, he's no farm dog," said brother Bob.

He wasn't a "farm dog" for sure. Farm dogs are generally "mixed breed." Heck, fact is that's being kind, they're no breed at all, just mongrels. This little stranger appeared to be, a not often encountered, purebred dog.

Uncle Leon and Mom apparently heard all the commotion and joined us in the yard to see what was going on. With their reasoned input we concluded somebody from Hutchinson, some ten miles distance, must have dumped the pup down our dusty road. Whoever, they must have been in dire straights to have given up such a fine little specimen. Pup seemed to readily understand his challenge as he was doing his darndest to win us over.

"Look' it him bring me a stick."

"He wants you to throw it, go ahead!"

"Look' it him go by-golly!"

Uncle Leon, thumbs tucked under the straps of his bib overalls, one bushy eyebrow raised said, "We don't need another mouth to feed around here."

"He won't eat much, just table scraps."

Uncle Leon, "Better check with Shep on that."

Shep, also a "mixed breed" former stray was the then sole resident farm dog.

The little pup's performance worked and inside of fifteen minutes of arrival he had found a new home.

"Gotta have a name." Imaginatively, we came up with, Skippy.

Shep did come along to sniff out Skippy, who apparently passed the smell test, or maybe Shep just didn't see the little stranger as a threat. Anyway, Shep turned to his own affairs and trotted off with that slight limp he acquired when he almost had a rear paw sliced off by the hay mower the year before. Shep licked his paw reasonably well.

Skippy, evidently not yet realizing he had achieved residency status, kept up the jumping to and fro, lick, lick, lick, a little dog yelp, and chasing after the tail that was hardly there. By evening, when he was served a little pan of table scraps, he surely knew he had found a new home.

By the second day of residency things started to get interesting for the city turned farm dog.

My sister Sal and I were sitting on the front room floor arguing over checkers when suddenly we were jolted by a shrill, "Look at Skippy, look at Skippy. He's gonna die!" We jumped up, scattering board and checkers, bolted through the screen door to the front yard. Well, apparently in Skippy's previous life in town he hadn't encountered an ant hill of the humongous prairie variety. One thing no creature great or small wants to do is sniff-out an ant hill. Skippy's little snout was swollen to twice its normal size and you could tell, he was hurtin'.

Cousin Howard was shouting, "What'a we do? What'a we do?" As he ran to the shop to fetch Uncle Leon who arrived post haste.

I said, "We gotta take him to the doctor Uncle Leon!"

"Richard, this isn't St. Louis. Out here we don't take dogs to the doctor. He's got a little poison in his head and it'll simmer down and out." And, it did after a day or so, though for a while we kids thought curiosity was certainly going to kill the dog.

One hot day some of us kids decided, as we often did, to cool down by squirting each other with the hose. No more than underway when into the showering deluge ran Skippy with a stick in his mouth, darting in and out of the hose stream, daring the hoser to try and hit him. He'd played this game before. He was soon the center of attention and we kids were only catching the residual spray. We finally tired, had cooled off a bit, and shut the hose down to drip dry. But Skippy apparently hadn't had enough as he trotted off, rear-end left of center, and headed straight for the barnyard cattle tank and to the astonishment of two slurping Holsteins jumped in and began dog paddling around the tank. When his little legs apparently tired he managed to shimmy out of the tank to ground followed by the obligatory full body shake. The cows looking on incredulously.

Over the next few weeks Skippy met up with the jumbo Kansas jack rabbits that had to be conflicted as to who should be chasing whom.

Uncle Leon reported that when he went down to slop the hogs one day Skippy tagged along and observed what the pigs had for dinner. Uncle Leon said it was the only time he could recall seeing a dog retch over a hog trough. A city dog thing we figured.

Unfortunately for Skippy, and the rest of us as well, he met the tuxedo clad Mr. Skunk that elicited a bountiful pungent spray. We had to live with that lingering odor for a week or so despite giving him the home remedy tomato juice bath—which doesn't work.

The "fighting rooster" definitely got Skippy's number as Skippy honored the little red feather cloaked devil's territorial claim. I don't know why the fighting rooster was so angry as by only pure luck he was singled out to live solely to service fifteen to twenty hens on a whenever basis.

One day we heard a yip and a yup ruckus and went outside to find Skippy had encountered a five-foot bull snake with the back legs of a suffocating toad twitching from its mouth. Skippy would bark and charge, back off, bark and charge 'til finally the slippery serpent slithered off into the weeds with Skippy, standing motionless now with his head quizzically tilted slightly to the right, watching this strange creature move on to finish his meal in peace.

We only observed Skippy making one trip to the bull pen. He crouched and peered under the board fence and when the hulking brown, black eyed, snot dripping bull glared back at him and began pawing the dusty ground with his right front hoof, Skippy did a quick 180 and exited, as far as we know never to return.

One day Skippy came running and barking into the farmyard appearing to be trying to tell us something. He would charge towards us then go in reverse as if he were trying to lead us somewhere. My cousin Hal and I ultimately followed him and he led us a few hundred yards into the pasture where we discovered what all the fuss was about. There was Opal, a roan cow, big brown eyes bulging, lying there on her side in the grass, unmoved by our approach, and nearby a recently delivered, obviously dead, calf. We ran back up to the farmyard to fetch Uncle Leon who hurried to the scene. Opal surely knew her calf was dead, but now raised to her feet, bent her head down and gave the calf a couple swipes with her tongue and slowly, somewhat unsteadily, walked away.

Uncle Leon asked Hal and me to bury the carcass. I went up to the tool shed, got a couple shovels, and returned to where the little brown and white calf lay. Hal and I dug about a three-foot deep hole, Skippy circling us the whole time, and deposited the calf, covered it with dirt and went home.

A couple days later we were in town and bumped into my Uncle "Tiny" Tyson, my dad's brother who lived in town. We told him our story about the calf. He told us it was interesting, but too bad we buried the calf before skinning it as the skin could be worth a lot of money. Bingo! Hal and I couldn't wait to get back to the farm as we hurried Mom and Aunt Emma through the grocery shopping. Back at the farm, the car still rolling to a stop, Hal and I jumped out, grabbed a couple shovels from the tool shed and headed for the pasture gravesite. We frantically started to dig and quickly came upon the carcass. We lifted same out and laid it on the ground. Skippy had come with us to the grave site, but at this point he turned around and headed home. Seen enough I guess. We both now had our pocket knives out and open. Hal was bigger than me and said I should go first. We had some discussion about how to go about the skinning and came up with him holding the calf's legs upward so I was looking at the calf's belly. I moved in and made the first incision and then we alternated cutting as we progressed. Slice, peel. slice, peel. A messy business. It was a good hour before we had the skin free and clear.

We re-buried the carcass.

It was a few days before we were in town again so we could visit the hide and skin shop. Mom wasn't happy about hauling the skin in her car as it had taken on a bit of an aroma, but allowed it in the trunk. Arriving in town Hal and I rushed to the skin place and offered our trophy skin to the proprietor. We got sixty cents for it. That might not sound like much, but this was the mid-forties and that was good for about six bottles of pop each. Not too bad.

We don't know how Skippy got his left ear mangled. Possibly tried to make friends with wily coyote. If so, bad call.

We couldn't have been happier with Skippy nor he, I suspect, with us. Then one early morning, disaster struck. I was still curled up in bed when a blood curdling scream blew through the front door. Mom was in the kitchen and my siblings were in various stages of rising. We all darted to and out the front door where cousin Jill was screaming, "Look, look, Skippy! He won't get up!" Little Skippy was absolutely still. Within a few minutes the whole farm clan had clustered around the front stoop of our house.

Uncle Leon bent down for a closer look and gave Skippy a little, "any life there?" push in the belly—"Skippy's gone, Skippy's dead."

Skippy lay on his side on the concrete stoop, legs stiffly out front, protruding half-inch of now pinkish tongue pinched between his little yellow teeth, eyes closed. He was gone all right. Didn't know how or why.

Uncle Leon said, "He's gotta be buried soon."

We kids were all in a state of shock, but somehow to mask true emotion, someone offered a diversionary, "I know, let's give Skippy an honest to goodness dog funeral!"

"Great idea," with forced levity, we all agreed.

After considering various alternatives we decided on a burial plot under the big shade tree back by the play saloon.

We all took an assignment in gathering the proper funeral paraphernalia. He was a little dog so didn't need much of a casket; an old wooden egg crate would do. The casket to be lined with an old worn-out blue denim work shirt from the rag bag.

A grave digging detail was dispatched. There would be an old wooden cross. Not too big, but big enough. Some freshly picked sunflowers poised in a Mason jar would be nice.

After collecting all the necessary props and everyone had completed their particular task, we were ready to proceed with the service. We all made our way back to where Skippy lay prostrate on the concrete stoop. We looked at each other quizzically and finally oldest brother Dan, the rock, said, "I'll put him in the casket," and lifted Skippy, now semi-rigor-mortised, and gently laid him in the improvised casket, draped the denim over his little body, closed the top of the egg crate casket and clicked shut the little wire clasp.

The previously agreed upon pallbearers lifted the casket and began a slow stutter step procession as we others fell in line. Someone started us on the customary—"Dum, Dum, DeDum, Dum, DeDum, Dum, Dum, Dum, Dum." It was a solemn and respectful procession.

From beginning to Skippy's final resting place we traversed about 500 feet—across our front yard, down the dirt path to the back of our cousins' house, and out to the area of the saloon and the cottonwood shade tree. The ready grave was about three feet deep with a mound of fresh dirt along side. An old wooden cross stood at the head with the Mason jar of yellow sunflowers adjacent. The pallbearers gently laid the casket in the grave as we all gathered 'round. Someone said, "We forgot about words, somebody has to say words."

We hadn't noticed Uncle Leon had slipped up to observe the going on's until he said, "I will." He stepped towards the grave, doffed his old straw hat, with head bowed, and warmth, said simply, "Skippy, it was a short summer for you, but it will be a long winter for us, amen." He then bent down and picked up a handful of the fresh dirt, dropped it in the open grave, turned, and walked back towards the barn to get back to farming. One by one, following his lead, we each shuffled over picked up and dropped a fistful of dirt in the grave. As I did so I gave my thigh an emotion avoiding diversionary pinch with one hand as I dropped dirt with the other.

The service over I stepped back, and hoping inconspicuously, crept away from the burial ground and around the corner of our cousins' house. As I glanced back for a last look Dan was shoveling the remaining dirt on the grave and the others were slipping away; it seemed no twos, everyone apparently going his or her own way. I never had occasion to count the little private spots around the farm, but there apparently were at least ten.

I walked out towards the granary, went around back, sat

down on the ground, and as my butt hit the ground the tears hit my cheeks. With my first sob I momentarily lost my breath to a burst of emotion; why Skippy, why Skippy, what did little Skippy do? He was such a joy. I hoped it was quick. I just didn't understand it. I sat grieving for a good hour not reaching any plausible understanding as to why this happened to Skippy, regained my composure as best I could, and walked back towards home and the comfort of family.

The kids hadn't re-congregated in the farmyard so I went to the house to ostensibly check with Mom about lunch. As I passed through the kitchen Mom turned from the stove momentarily and gave my arm a squeeze. Brother Bob was sitting at the kitchen table whistling and I noticed that his eyes were reddened. I slipped into the bathroom, looked in the mirror and saw my eyes were red too, so splashed a little rejuvenating cold water on my face and went on to face the sometimes cruel harsh world.

In a couple days, normalcy seemed to return to the farm. We didn't talk much about Skippy after that. I know it wasn't that he wasn't thought about, rather I think no one wanted to be suspected of showing much sentimentality over a silly little dog we hardly knew. But Uncle Leon was right—it would be a long winter.

Though only nine years old the summer of the Skippy incident I learned something I hoped I'd remember for the rest of my life. I hoped we had expressed enough affection for Skippy when he was alive, as we surely did, when he died.

END

Escape from Babylon

It was slow for a Saturday night at the Starlight Roof. The eight o'clock show was over. Management called it a Broadway Review which featured a comedian/impersonator, a boy/girl duo singing show tunes, and a short line of knock-out chorus girls. The Starlight Roof was the home of the Chase Club and companion Zodiac Lounge atop the Chase Hotel in midtown St. Louis "overlooking beautiful Forest Park." The Chase Club was first-tier and featured artists such as Frankie Laine and Martin and Lewis and a radio talk-show broadcast from the Zodiac Lounge. The club and lounge's south and west walls were floor to ceiling plate glass offering a panoramic view of mid-town St. Louis and Forest Park while the clubs north side held the stage and the east side billowing tapestry. The night-like ceiling in the club, with an assist from Union Electric, twinkled stars.

The Chase Club's tall handsome tuxedo clad maitre d's name was Hack. The boys didn't know if that was a first name, a last name, or a nickname. In Club hierarchy, it was really of no consequence, as it was not likely there would be occasion for any dialogue between a maitre d'and a lowly busboy.

Rob and Joe bused dinner tables at the Chase Club for the mostly Greek waiters six 'til eleven for a presumed ten-percent cut of the waiters tips. Rob and Joe were always skeptical as to the waiters mathematical aplomb, but the presumed tip share plus minimum wage, a passable supper included, made for decent summer jobs for two seventeen year old suburbanites in a 50's summer pending their fall departure for Columbia and Mizzou. Keeping water glasses full, and cleaning off and re-setting tables, though humbling, didn't require a lot of physical nor brain power. It was a job the boys could handle.

Rob and Joe operated quite differently. Rob liked to spend what idle moments he had backstage flirting with the showgirls. He also took to the impersonator and ultimately did a better job on Walter Brennan than the performer, but he couldn't nail down a decent Jimmy Stewart or James Cagney—not even close. Joe, on the other hand, was very adept at working the customers for extra tips. He could be particularly attentive and affable. One evening a visiting Detroit gangster and his lady friend were so taken with Joe and his charm that they had the photo-gal take a big-smiles picture of the threesome, a print for each, and the hood tipped Joe twenty dollars—not bad in those days.

Rob was fired twice—once for simple ineptitude at the job and the other time because one of the showgirls inexplicably demanded it. There was one Greek busboy, about twenty-five, the boys called "super-bus" whose exemplary table work made an ordinary, to sub-ordinary, bus like Rob look bad. Both times Rob was fired a few days after Joe was able to talk management into bringing him back on a "last warning" basis. After all, the Club didn't have a lot of guys standing in line for bus-boy jobs.

The dinner crowd was thin after the second show so Angelo, the waiters captain, cut Rob and Joe loose around ten pm. Now ten pm was early for a couple of guys that ordinarily slept 'til noon and it WAS Saturday night. They went through the "whatta you wanna do's" and, exercising their customary poor judgment, they decided in short order to make the trip over the Mississippi to the much maligned, yet undeniably sleazy, East St. Louis, Illinois. Joe had a 41 Ford coupe that got about twenty-five miles to the gallon of gas, and about ten miles to the quart of oil. They punched out on the time clock and were soon in Joe's car, spewing a trail of black soot, traveling east for Eads Bridge and the Land of Lincoln.

Joe switched on the radio broadcast from the Zodiac Lounge and picked up Jonnie Ray weeping his way through *Cry.*

About mid-Eads Bridge Joe queried, "Where you wanna go first?"

Rob responded, "How about the Palladium?"

"Sounds good."

The Palladium was an reputed mob controlled Dixieland

Jazz club featuring the Singleton Palmer band. Palmer and his band had been part of the music scene around St. Louis for many years.

The boys earlier in the summer had become chummy with one of the Palladium's bouncers, Mickey the Moocher, a/k/a Mickey Moose, but there had been some inter-mob difficulties on the East Side over the last several weeks and bodies were popping out of Cadillac trunks including one, Mickey the Moocher. He would be missed.

The Palladium was packed as would be expected on a Saturday night. Being under twenty-one didn't account for much in East St. Louis as long as your height met the mark on the entrance door frame. Sorta like being tall enough to ride the roller coaster. The boys elbowed their way through the club and were fortunate enough to find a pedestal table towards the back and soon flagged a waitress and ordered a couple of Buds. They sat back, fingers and feet tapping, head bobbing, enjoying the music and the lively going-on's around them. The usual routine for closing the third set was for the band to leave the drummer on stage behind the bar while the rest of the band left the stage, in their red-vested riverboat garb, flat-top straw hats, and marched their way winding through the Palladium blasting *The Saints* while the club went wild. Bedlam perhaps, but great entertainment.

After about an hour at the Palladium Rob and Joe decided to move down the street to the more sedate Terrace Lounge, also reputed to be mob controlled.

The Terrace was featuring Illinois Jacquet the great tenor-sax man and his trio. Joe and Rob found a place at the bar, ordered beers, and enjoyed the man and his silky sax. The Terrace had a more subdued atmosphere than the Palladium. It was a narrow room with a long bar front-to-back with a small stage mid-bar—smoky, soft lights. With Dixieland the crowd becomes part of the action, with cool jazz the crowd does more listening, absorbing. When Jacquet did his signature number *Flying Home* a hush fell over the Terrace Lounge as the audience cooled out.

When the trio took a break Joe and Rob got to talking to a

fella sitting next to them at the bar that was particularly garrulous which they soon learned was because he'd just had a good evening at the Fairmont Racetrack and was flush with cash. His name was Dudley.

As the three were talking Rob got a tap on the shoulder and a tall slender gray haired bespectacled man who introduced himself as Sterling said he and his daughter Nancy were out celebrating her eighteenth birthday and they'd sure be pleased if the boys would join them at their table and partake in the celebration.

Rob turned to Joe—Joe shrugged his shoulders—"Why not."

So the boys moved to Sterling and Nancy's table and Sterling ordered the table a round of drinks. Dudley still at the bar kept glancing their way with that "why not me" look on his face 'til the boys asked Sterling if he'd mind if Dudley also joined the table and Sterling said he had no objection so they motioned Dudley and his big grin to join them. Intros all around.

Nancy was a cute little blue-eyed brunette who clearly took to Rob and insisted that he sit next to her, which pleased Rob, but clearly astonished Joe because he ordinarily was the lady-charmer.

The table was again enjoying Illinois Jacquet and the conversation was lively, if not stimulating. Nancy had just graduated from East St. Louis High School, Sterling worked maintenance at Granite City Steel, Dudley's winning horse was Bonnie Lad, and all were from tipsy to loaded.

As the trio finished their next set, Sterling popped up with, "Why don't we all get out'a here and go over to our place?"

Rob and Joe exchanged curious glances and Joe said, "Sure, why not."

As Dudley now belonged to the group he tagged along with Rob and Joe as they made their way out of the Terrace and towards Joe's car. They connected with Sterling and his car, proceeded ten or so blocks, pulled up in front of an old brick three story apartment building in a not so great neighborhood. They got out of their respective cars and fell in line behind Sterling and Nancy who led them up a concrete stoop, through an unlocked wood and glass panel door, up two flights of stairs and into a dingy Goodwill furnished apartment. Sterling was drunk, Dudley was drunk, Rob and Joe were tipsy and Nancy was enjoying an alcohol induced giddiness. Sterling, thankfully, made no offer of drinks and stumbled across the room, struggled with a record player, and managed to put on a Glenn Miller record. Dudley parked on the floor with his now permanent smile and kept muttering, "Go Bonnie Lad, go Bonnie Lad." The unlikely five-some were all talking, or babbling foolishly.

Nancy and Rob found their way to the kitchen and moved along to the semi-secluded side of the refrigerator trying to contort their bodies into a meaningful relationship; all to Glen Miller's *Stardust*. Nancy was anxious, Rob was willing, but suddenly Rob's ear nibbling was interrupted by a KER-BANG! coming from the other room.

"What the hell!"

Rob scurried from the kitchen to the other room in the apartment to see Sterling had pulled a Murphy bed from the wall and slammed it to the floor and was hopping around the room, trying to balance himself while undressing, one pants leg off the other on—all to Glenn Miller's *American Patrol*.

THUMP, THUMP, THUMP.

Joe had backed wide-eyed into a corner and when he saw Rob he shouted, "Let's get the hell out'a here!" Rob took a last "if only" look at Nancy who responded with a menacing frown. As Rob and Joe bolted for the door, Dudley, still sitting on the floor, pleaded, "What about me?" Joe scooted over, grabbed Dudley by the arm, "Com'on partner, we're out'a here."

"Happy Birthday," and out the door as Sterling, all tangled in his pants legs, finally stumbled to the floor.

The threesome made it out of the apartment building and to Joe's car. Once in, "What the hell was that thump, thump, thump?" wondered Rob.

"I think that was their downstairs neighbor thumping on

their ceiling with a broomstick," Joe surmised.

Joe asked, "Dudley, where do we park you?"

Dudley, still smiling and babbling about his winnings, said, "Just get me to the State Hotel, State Hotel, just get me there."

The boys knew the hotel which was located on the main drag in downtown East St. Louis and were pulling up in front in about ten minutes.

Rob hopped out, pulled forward the seat back, grabbed Dudley by the arm, and pulled him to the sidewalk.

Joe said, "Better steady him and lead him in."

"OK." Rob took Dudley's elbow and led him through the hotel entrance into a dingy poorly lit lobby. Rob noticed the head of an old man dozing in a grungy overstuffed leather chair where the cushion was either missing or had been squashed flat by age as it looked like at any moment the old geezer was going to be sinking right through the floor. They moved to the front desk—no clerk in sight so Rob ding-dinged the desk bell—a clerk appeared from an open doorway behind the desk. The guy was an albino. His hair and his skin were as white as Aunt Polly's fence and his eyes had a pinkish hue. Someone into color coordination would certainly have told him not to have worn the white shirt.

Rob said, "This fella wants a room for the night, no luggage, he's got the money."

The clerk looked them up and down for a spell, hesitated, and then asked Rob, "Is he all right? I mean is he sick or something? He don't look so good—and tell him to stop staring at me like that!"

"Naw, he's fine, just had a few too many—he'll be all right—promise."

"OK, sign in here," as the clerk's milky hand pushed a pad towards Dudley, and "That'll be twelve dollars."

The clerk slid a key over the counter towards Dudley, "Third floor, number 304."

Dudley managed to make his mark and peeled twelve dollars off his still fat roll of bills and paid the clerk. Rob led Dudley to the elevator and nudged him in, poked his head in, pushed the three button, pulled out and was saying, "Sleep well Dudley" as the elevator door closed.

Rob quickly exited the hotel and got in the curbside coupe. As the door closed Joe said, "Where to now?"

"WHAT!, are you nut? Let's get the hell out'a here!"

Joe lamented, "But it's early. How about we stop by McGarvy's?"

McGarvy's was one of the whorehouses on the East Sides red-light strip. Rob and Joe would stop at McGarvy's once in a while on their East Side excursions, not to indulge, rather just to watch the whores work the crowd while they nursed a beer or two.

Rob relented, "OK, what the hell, we can sleep in the morning."

"That's my boy."

They were in front of McGarvy's in about ten minutes, parked the car, got out, and walked in. McGarvy's appeared to be a run-of-the-mill tavern, except the lighting wasn't as subdued as in most taverns, and a half a dozen "ladies" were milling about plying their trade to about a like number of guys. Rob and Joe found a table, sat and ordered a couple of beers from the waitress, and began perusing the house for anything interesting. Rob observed that perhaps the table was cleaned off nicely, but the floor was a little sticky and the aroma of stale beer hovered all around.

"Hey," Joe responded, "where in the rules does it say a whorehouse has to be pristine? Next thing you know you'll be expecting the scent of roses and clean sheets."

There was a sign on the wall behind the bar—WE DON'T SERVE SCOTCH.

Pointing to the wall, "What's that all about?" queried Joe.

"I don't know," said Rob—"maybe it means don't get uppity in here."

They weren't there long before a young lady, probably about twenty, approached their table and asked if they'd buy her a drink. Joe spoke up, "Sure, sit, what's your name?"

She ordered a glass of Champagne and introduced herself as "Scarlett".

"As in O'Hara?" Joe asked.

"Yea, you got a problem with that?"

"No-No."

Joe engaged Scarlett in conversation while Rob's attention was drawn to an old, probably at least fifty, whore at the bar who was working on an older gentleman. She was being especially lively and demonstrative, selling somewhat aggressively what little sex-appeal she clung to.

Scarlett didn't waste much time before inquiring as to the boys interest in moving upstairs.

"How much?" Joe inquired.

"Three dollars."

Rob noticed activity at the bar where the old whore was now on her feet, a big smile on her face, and hand in hand was leading the old guy through the curtain draped doorway at the rear of the bar.

"Three dollars?" Joe confirmed. "I don't know. Rob and I will talk it over."

Scarlett said, "It'd be the most enjoyable three dollars you ever spent—don't keep me waiting now," as she stood and strolled off.

She was kinda cute, but Rob commented that when she smiled you could see one of her front teeth was broken in half. She sorta had one and a half front teeth. It may also have been a few days since she last washed her hair—but, not too bad.

Joe said, "Well whata you think?"

"Whata you mean, whata I think?"

Joe said, "Don't you think it's about time? You know you'll be eighteen on your next and you gotta get some soon and I don't see why tonight can't be the night. How about that one down at the end of the bar in the leopard-skin outfit? Not bad, huh?"

"Ya gotta be kiddin', look at her, you can't tell where the leopard-skin ends and her skin begins—forget it!"

"Then how about that one mid-bar with the milky skin and red hair? She looks nice."

"Ya right, her skin's the color of day-old bread and her

hair's the color of an over ripe pumpkin."

"You're sure fussy," retorted Joe.

"Maybe if they turned the lights down a bit."

"Hey Rob, you aint exactly a whores dream, ya know."

"You're so anxious, why don't you get some tonight?"

"I've already had some."

Maybe Joe had, maybe he hadn't.

Rob suggested, "Why don't we both go upstairs."

Joe responded, "How much money you got?"

Rob said, "Four bucks."

"Well," Joe said, "I got three, but we'll owe that for the beers and Scarlett's glass of Champagne."

"Whata you mean Champagne, I know Ginger Ale when I see it."

Rob said, "Why don't we flip a coin to see who goes upstairs?"

"Naw," said Joe, "If only one can go it stands to reason it should to be you—ya'aint never been before."

"I'm not so sure you've done the deed before Joe."

"Sure have."

Influenced by the beer, and the all to brief amorous interlude with Nancy, Rob was vulnerable. Maybe his time had come.

"OK," said Rob. "I'll do it."

Joe located Scarlett across the bar gave her the "over here" hand signal and she sashayed over to the table and Joe took it upon himself to tell her his friend was ready to go upstairs.

There was that tooth and a half smile—"You won't be sorry."

She took Rob's hand and led him towards and through the curtain draped archway to the back staircase. She hadn't noticed, and neither did Rob, that Joe was tagging along. As she got to the third step up she turned and saw Joe and said, "Where the hell do you think you're going?"

Joe replied, "I've got an investment in this venture so I oughta at least be able to watch."

Scarlett said, "Oh no you don't, get out'a here!"

"No!"

Scarlett shouted in the direction of the barroom, "Bruiser, we got a problem in here!"

"Brusier?"

Joe backed down the stairs and returned to the waiting room.

Scarlett re-took Rob's hands an said, "Com'along Sweet Pea."

Rob thought, *Sweet Pea? Where's she get off calling me sweet pea?—Snaggle-tooth!*

They walked up to the second floor landing and walked down a darkened hall past a couple of closed doors and came to an open third. She led Rob into a room that was about twelve by twelve with faded blue flowered wallpaper, a drop cord supporting a single light bulb, a washstand with a pan of water and washcloth atop, a straight-back wooden chair and a cot-sized bed not covered in a clean white sheet, but rather what looked like a gray oil-cloth.

Scarlett said, "Drop your pants so I can take a look."

Rob thought, *Take a look? Aren't they pretty much all alike? Take a look?*

The rather embarrassing clinical part, that Rob hadn't been warned about, came next, after which she said he was OK.

He thought, *Of course I'm OK—What the hell about you?* But he let it go.

She asked for and got his three dollars and pulled her shift over her head, no panties, left her bra on, laid down on the bed and said, "OK kiddo, get to it."

After six to ten seconds the first time in a lifetime was all over.

She pushed Rob off, rolled off the bed and said, "Get your pants on," as she squatted and tended to herself. When they were dressed she didn't take Rob's hand, rather just clasped his elbow and led him back to and down the steps, through the curtained doorway, to the barroom.

Rob had taken just a few steps across the barroom floor when he was startled by a shrill "hey-you" whistle. Rob stopped, looked towards the bar where the whistle came from and the lady whistler, looking at Rob, pointed to the floor to Rob's rear, and said, "Are those yours sonny?"

Rob turned, looked to the floor, and there were his white Jockey underpants, appearing to have been dipped in luminous dye, lying crumpled on the middle of the barroom floor.

A rapturous laughter and whistles quickly erupted from the motley group of whores and their patrons and of course Rob recognized the loudest laugh of all coming from his good friend Joe. He could sense his face turning a prickly red. Rob hurriedly stepped back, reached down, scooped up his underpants, stuffed them into a pocket, and was quickly out the front door, the laughter persisting behind.

Obviously, afterwards upstairs, alcohol impaired, Rob didn't manage to get back into his Jockeys, they got hung-up in a pants leg, then dropped out to the floor at a most inopportune time.

HUMILLATING!

Rob quickly found the car and watched impatiently for Joe who soon came out of McGarvy's door and down the sidewalk towards the car still laughing, though reduced to a respectful giggle as he approached Rob and the car.

"Not funny Joe."

"Oh, be a sport Rob. Could have happened to me, or anybody."

"It didn't though, did it Joe? Let's get out'a here NOW!"

They got into the car and Joe drove in the direction of the Mississippi, escaping from Babylon, as the old Ford black-belched its way towards Eads Bridge and home.

"Well, my first time certainly wasn't what you'd call beautiful."

"No, but it certainly was what you'd call memorable."

"Go to hell."

"Do you 'wanna stop for a minute so you can put your Jockey's back on?"

"Shut-up."

Joe turned on the radio and caught the Zodiac Lounge at closing time playing, *show me the way to go home—I'm tired and I wanna go to bed—had a little drink....*

Rob and Joe finished out the summer as busboys uneventfully at the Chase Club and wisely passed on any more trips east of the Mississippi. That's not to say they didn't find a little mischief on the west side of the river that summer, but not the debauchery they found on the east side of the river.

For the rest of that summer, sometimes when Rob and Joe were together, for no apparent reason Joe would start to giggle. Rob knew damn well what Joe was giggling about and asked him to kindly "knock it off!" That being said, as far as Rob could discern, Joe kept the nefarious incident between the two of them. On the other hand it was a given that the folks at McGarvy's would be talking about the night of the skinny kid and the errant Jockey shorts for some time to come.

END

The Christmas Coin

It was a bitterly cold and damp Saturday in late December. It made little difference how many layers of clothing you put on; the cold penetrated to the bone. He had about a ten-block trek to his job at the NEWS DEPOT. The wind-driven sleet was whipping at his face encrusting his eyebrows in ice. He crinkled his toes in his boots but nonetheless could feel them cold and damp. Fortunately, his mother had collared him before he got out the door with "here, for goodness sakes, put on this stocking cap, scarf, and here's your gloves— you're going to catch your death young man." Now, in route, he'd pulled the cap down over his ears hopeful they wouldn't fall off before he reached the warmth of the store. He was thankful, though, for his treasured warm blue wool-and-nylon RAMS jacket.

The NEWS DEPOT was located right on the town square between Arnold's jewelry store and Abbott's pharmacy. The stock in trade consisted of local and regional newspapers, magazines, several racks of paperback books, coffee, candy, tobacco, and possibly most importantly, lottery tickets.

Tom Dooley had been the proprietor of the NEWS DEPOT for the past ten years. He was a balding, medium build man but for a pot belly, probably about fifty with half glasses generally perched at the tip of his rather bulbous nose. He had what might be described as a typical shopkeepers demeanor—a cheerful, "Good morning" and a parting "Have a good one." He was surely sick to death of people walking through the door with a "Hang down your head Tom Dooley," and laughing as if they were the first with this clever salutation.

Due to the miserable weather Bill was a few minutes late for work. Saturdays he worked 8AM to1PM and Monday through Friday, after school, 3PM 'til closing at 6PM.

As Bill hurried through the door, Tom said, "Boy, you look like a waif's been lost in the artic."

Bill shivered, stomped the ice from his boots, brushed the snow from his jacket and said, "Sorry I'm late, weather slowed me down, but I'll make it up."

"Not necessary," said Tom, "Heck, I'm impressed you're here at all. I only hope you thaw out by spring; you aint exactly purty with them purple lips and nose."

Tom would fall into that stern-but-fair category. He paid Bill a dollar over minimum wage which was fair, but there was to be zero idle time, which was stern. It wasn't always easy not to appear idle in the News Depot. How many times could you straighten the magazine rack, dust the shelves, freshen the coffee, or sweep the floor? Whatever, they had an agreeable employer/employee not master/servant relationship.

Bill really didn't know too much about Tom: divorced, lived alone, and apparently had a daughter he rarely heard from that lived somewhere in the East.

Bill got to know several of the regulars and there were some real Pips. Both the City Hall and the Courthouse were nearby, so he got to know the mayor who came in every afternoon for a newspaper and a couple cigars. He never lit the cigars, just chewed the tips to a repulsive gooey mush. The lawyers came and went pulling behind huge briefcases atop little wheeled carriers inferring they were working on something really big. Tom would say, "Somebody's misery packed in them bags." The real estate lady with what Tom called the big bazooms came in for cigarettes and lottery tickets a couple times a week. Tom's line was, "You know why that lady always looks like she's leaning backwards? Because she's afraid if she leans forwards she'll tip over!"

Recently one of the magazine distributors brought in a sales rack of quarter collecting boards for the new state-by-state highlighting quarters. It was a rigid cardboard about a foot square with round slots to insert the quarters. The board sold for two dollars. Bill thought coin-collecting sounded like a good hobby and as he had ready access to a flow of quarters he figured it wouldn't take him too long to fill a board with the quarters minted to date. Any quarter he took from the cash drawer he'd of course replace with one from his own pocket. Tom had no problem with the plan as long as Bill paid for the collection board up front. So, Bill began his new hobby and soon filtered through incoming quarters for six states.

Bill's dad had clerked at a downtown hardware store until the store was squeezed out by a Home Depot that opened out at the edge of town. When the lights went on at the Home Depot they went off at Smith's Hardware. Mr. Mueller was in his fourth week of unemployment and had his application in several places, but to date, no luck.

Mr. Mueller announced at dinner one recent evening that what he'd really like to do is become a barber. He'd spoken about this with his barber who had an empty chair and was encouraged that the barber had said he'd be happy to bring him on board. The only obstacle was Mr. Mueller didn't have a barber's license, nor the tuition money for barber college. So, the prospect was only a dream.

Their white wavy aluminum siding duplex, with the fake green shutters, was comfortable enough and not unlike most of the other homes on the block, all of which dated to the 50's. Bill and his little brother Gil shared a room with oak bunk beds, dresser drawers, with Bill getting the top two drawers and his little brother the bottom two.

There were Albert Pujols and Marc Bulger posters on the red ("if that's what you want, that's what you'll get") walls. The glass globe on the ceiling light fixture was long gone leaving a naked 75 watt bulb as the sole room light.

Their mother was a good housekeeper and the home was always clean and tidy. She prided herself in being one of those "stay at home moms" and her boys always had clean clothes on their backs and, though maybe not the most expensive cuts, food on the table.

With Christmas coming on it didn't promise to be particularly merry. Mrs. Mueller told the boys, "The gifts this year may be a little skimpy, but wait'til next year." The money Bill brought home from the News Depot certainly helped and Mr. Mueller got a temp job at a nursery garden selling Christmas trees at a dollar commission per.

Bill was making progress on filling his quarters board and had twenty states covered. It was the Wednesday before Christmas, which fell on a Saturday, and as he scanned the quarters in the cash drawer he eyed a Massachusetts which he didn't yet have. He was about to slip it into the boards coin slot when something caught his eye. He took a closer look at the state identity side and there was something about the Minute Man and his musket that just didn't look quite right. He eye-balled it closer and it looked to him like there were two over-lapping Minute Men. Like there was one man piggy-backing the other. Plus there was a ding on the coin edge. He wondered what had happened there—it wasn't right.

"Tom, take a look at this coin; the soldiers are piggy-backing—isn't that weird?"

Tom took a look, "Get me that magnifying glass out'a the drawer."

Tom studied the coin, then lowered the glass. "This is strange isn't it. Never seen anything like that before. Maybe the coin's worth something, never know. Why maybe could be worth twenty, twenty-five dollars."

"You really think that could be?" reacted Bill.

"Well, could be. Tell you what I'm going over to St. Louis tomorrow on some business and I've got a friend over there that owns a coin shop. I've got the time so why don't I stop by and show the coin to him and see what you've got there."

"Would you do that Tom?"

"Sure."

So Bill gave Tom the coin and Tom did get over to St. Louis on Wednesday. He took care of his business and as expected had the time to stop by his friend's coin shop so the shopkeeper could take a look at Bill's coin. Tom made his way to the shop and went in to find his friend, Frank, the shop owner. They exchanged greetings.

"Tom how's it going?—long time no see—what brings you to my humble little shop? Didn't know you were interested in numismatics."

"Well Frank, I've got a coin I'd like you to take a look at. Probably nothing, but it looks to be a little different."

Tom pulled the quarter from his pocket, handed it to Frank, "Look how that soldier, or whatever, seems to be doubled-up; looks like the one kinda melds into the other one."

"Lem'me get my glass," said Frank. After a brief examination he said, "No it's not right. It's what's called an overstrike. You see somehow at the mint, Philadelphia in this case, the press struck that coin twice; most likely a mechanical failure. That happens once in a while, but it's almost always caught before the coins leave the mint and they're destroyed. I saw an item about this coin in COIN TALK a week or so ago. Seems they discovered the overstrike, but somehow about ten found their way into circulation. Your coin's worth real money to a serious numismatist."

"How much?"

"I really don't know, let me make a call to a dealer friend in New York," as he moved to his inner-office leaving Tom to ponder what he'd just heard.

In a few minutes Frank came back out—"I've been authorized to offer you $5000 for your coin."

Frank, gasping, "$5000! Holy Moly!"

"Yea", Frank said, "Like I'd recalled there were only ten of those coins that made it into circulation. That makes it very rare."

Tom responded, "I don't have to think long about that—I'll take it."

"Well all right," said Frank, "I assume a check's OK?"

"Yea, check's OK—Just make it out to cash though."

(*Tom's mind scrambled—$5000—a lot of money—but it's Bill's—it's my shop—my cash drawer—if I hadn't suggested that I check with Frank, Bill would have just put it in his coin board and forgotten about it—heck, fifty dollars could make Bill happy—maybe two-fifty*).

Frank made out the check and handed it to Tom, "Here ya' are. I'm glad you thought of me. Be careful now that check's same as cash ya' know."

"Yea, thanks Frank"—and as he moved to the door—"and need I say, great to do business with you."

"Don't be a stranger," Frank said, as the shop door closed.

Tom retrieved his car from the parking lot and headed over the river for home. He had a lot of thinking to do.

(*Five thousand dollars—that's a hell of a lot of money. I've never had that much in my hands at one time before. Heck, Bill is just a kid—his whole life ahead of him. A sharp kid too. He'll probably go to college, law school, become a big lawyer or something—make a lot of money. But, I'm fifty-five, the dies been cast, I'll never really hit it big; did OK, but nothing really big. I'm due for a break—things haven't exactly gone my way. Trained as a machinist and now running a damned newsstand. My wife left me for another man fifteen years ago and my daughter blamed me for the break-up. Yea, I'm due for a break. Maybe it was just fate, maybe it's my turn, a natural phenomenon, yea, but maybe it was fate for the kid, maybe it's his shot. The coin thing was the kids idea. I wouldn't face this dilemma at all if the kid hadn't found that coin. And, he is a good kid, been a good worker, nice family. Yea, I got some thinking to do.*)

Tom had a restless night. (*Maybe I could take the $5000 dollars and invest it shrewdly, double the money and then give Bill back the original $5000. But how do I explain where the money's been in the meantime? Wouldn't work.*)

It was a Thursday and Tom hadn't planned on getting to the store 'til about eleven. Bill was on Christmas vacation from school and was to open the News Depot that morning.

There was a light snowfall as Tom drove downtown. He parked his car, as every other day, on the lot down and across the street from the News Depot. He got out of the car, his mind still befuddled, and moved down the sidewalk towards the store.

He reached the crossing corner and stepped off the curb and as he took a second step, a car, maybe moving too fast for the snowy street, was heading right for him—he was going to get hit! Suddenly, in an instant, a young man in a

RAMS jacket was in front of him and pounced on Tom's chest with the flat of his hands knocking Tom backwards over the curb to flat on his backside on the sidewalk. The car braking but sliding by.

A couple walking the sidewalk rushed over—"Are you all right!?—you really took a tumble—lie still, we'll call 911."

Tom had the wind knocked out of him—he gasped for breath, "OK, OK, OK, where'd that kid go? where'd he go?"

"What kid?"

"The kid that knocked me down."

"We didn't see any kid?"

"I TELL YA' SOME KID IN A RAMS JACKET KNOCKED ME OUTTA THE WAY'A THAT CAR!"

The fella that had been driving the car quickly slid to a stop, jumped out of his car and ran towards the downed man—"Is he OK? He stepped right in front of me."

Tom, now in a sitting position, "Did you see that kid?"

"What kid?"

"THE KID that pushed me outta the way'a your car."

"I didn't see any kid, mister."

Tom now said, "Help me to my feet."

They helped him up, he looked himself over, brushed the snow off his backside and said "I'm OK, OK, thanks, I'll be movin' along—I'm OK."

The man from the car said, "If you're sure."

"I'm sure—you folks sure you didn't see that kid?"

The couple shrugged, "No kid—glad you didn't get hurt, be careful now."

"Yea, thanks"—and Tom, a little wobbly a'foot, looking both ways, crossed the street and walked towards the News Depot.

Tom's head was spinning (*I know I was pushed, I can still feel the hands impact on my chest and that kid...no couldn't be, but yea, that kid did have on a RAMS jacket—I saw it*).

As he arrived there were a couple of the regulars in the store he "good morning'd" and quickly looked to the coat rack behind the counter—there hung Bill's blue RAMS jacket.

Tom asked, "You been out Bill?"

"No, right here since I opened, why?"

"Oh, nothing, just thought I might have seen you down the street."

"Wasn't me."

Tom shed his coat and said, "I gotta sit a minute," and took a seat behind the counter.

Bill brought him a cup of coffee.

"Thanks."

Tom tried to clear his head (*Yes—no, no—yes, something happened out there, something super-natural, a miracle, aberration, awakening, whatever, something happened that can't be explained. But, whatever it was, he now knew one thing certain*)

"Bill I've got some good news for you."

"What's that?"

"You know that quarter. I had my friend in St. Louis take a look at it yesterday. It's what they call an over-strike and some coins got out'a the mint before it was discovered. Makes it very rare and collectors pay big money for'em. He was willing to pay $5000 for it—I took it," and handed Bill the check.

"$5000! HOLY COW! Oh my gosh, Oh my gosh." As he glared at the check he held in his trembling hands. "I can't believe it."

"Well, believe it Bill, believe it. Now that checks made out for cash—you have an account over at City National— get yourself right over to that bank and get it deposited—go ahead now."

"Yea, right," as Bill grabbed his jacket, and with one arm down a sleeve, was out the door—Tom calling after, "Be careful, it's slippery out there."

Tom sat down again and sighed (*I feel pretty good—that kid's sure happy and I'm happy for him. Most importantly I learned something this morning, not least of which, that boy may have saved my life—in a couple ways.*)

Bill was of course anxious to get home and tell his family about their good fortune. They were all quite naturally in a prolonged state of disbelief. When they finally gathered their faculties they sat for a family meeting and decided: dad would get $3000 for tuition to barber college, mom a dish washer, Gil would get a new baseball glove, Tom Dooley would get $500 because, after all, the coin did come from his cash drawer and he found the buyer. That still left about $1000 for Bill's college savings account.

All the family members had a hard time getting to sleep that night, but that was all right.

Bill was scheduled to work 'til one o'clock when the store was to close for the holiday. It would be a white Christmas, although the snow was only about an inch deep. He made his way downtown and arriving at the News Depot happily greeted Tom, "Good morning and Merry Christmas."

Tom also seemed to be in an especially good mood— "Merry Christmas—called my daughter last night—she wants me to come for a visit right after the first of the year. She said we got a lot of catchin' up to do."

"That's great Tom, great, really great."

It was a slow morning customer-wise, but fast time-wise. About noon Tom said, "You get along now Bill, I'll close up."

"You sure?"

"Yea, I'm sure—now get out'a here."

As Bill walked out the door, he turned, "Oh yea, Mom said you should come over for Christmas dinner—may not be turkey, but it'll be good eats—around one."

Tom did have Christmas dinner with the Muellers. He reluctantly accepted a check for $500 as a Christmas gift.

They did have turkey—with all the trimmings.

END

The Elevator Incident

It was about eleven in the morning and the lobby of the Bradley Building was as usual bustling with people of all shapes and sizes coming and going, some in a hurry and others looking like they didn't care, or didn't know, where they were going. The Bradley Building was a fifteen-story steel and glass building about twenty years old that looked like countless other generic downtown buildings built in the same era. A coffee shop and a newsstand were located just off the lobby and there was a bank of four elevators to transport the workers and their visitors to and from their respective destinations. The building housed mostly professional tenants: lawyers, accountants, doctors and insurance firms.

Then, without any forewarning, the ordinary morning took an unordinary turn. The number four elevator was in a DOWN run between the fifth and fourth floor when it came to an abrupt, knee bending, halt. There were six people on board and when jolted to a stop they looked at each other with startled "What happened?" looks. No one among strangers said anything for a moment or so pondering "How much trouble am I in?"

A well dressed man in a blue pin-stripe suit, was the first to speak. "I'm an attorney here in the building and I've heard in the last week or so reports that there have been some problems with the elevators, but nothing major. I suspect we shouldn't be too long."

Another, "Too long, how long is that?"

"I'll tell you what, I'll get on the phone there and just make sure they know we've been stopped."

A young, kinda jumpy, woman passenger seemed alarmed and said, "Yes please, do something." With that the gentleman opened the little door at the control panel along side the door and IN THE CASE OF EMMERGENCY PUSH 0, and did so. Someone on the other end quickly answered and the gentleman told that person of the predicament.

The person on the other end said they were aware of the problem and would have someone on it right away.

Apparently it was just the number four elevator that had malfunctioned.

A fifty-ish man in a business suit, with some sarcasm, spoke up, "Why am I not surprised; stuck in an elevator; this makes my day just about perfect."

An attractive white haired woman said, "Now let's not get excited. I'm sure we'll be moving soon."

A teenage boy in jeans and sweat shirt, backwards baseball cap, with blond hair falling over his ears spoke up, "I gotta get outa here—my girlfriends waiting for me in the lobby. She hates it when I'm late."

"Oh, by all means do everything possible so the kid can get with his girlfriend before she gets upset. Call out the National Guard," said the sarcastic man.

The phone rang—the lawyer picked it up, "Yes?" The person on the other end reported they were on it, but it could take a while to get the necessary elevator service man on the scene and they'd stay in touch and tell us immediately when they had some news. "Well," hanging up, the lawyer said, "We may be a while so let's do the best we can to relax and pass the time—my name is Jim Brannon."

The sarcastic man spoke up "Great! This is just great. If anybody cares my name is Smith, as in just plain Smith. And if you detect that I'm just a little bit testy folks it's because fifteen minutes ago I lost my job because my boss said my sales results didn't meet expectations. Ten years on the job and this ninety-day wonder punk supervisor tells me my results didn't meet expectations. I shoulda quit a long ago."

The others were taken aback by the gentlemen's surprising brashness and after an awkward pause the older lady with the white hair said, "I'm awfully sorry to hear you lost your job, but I'd bet something will turn up soon. There's always a demand for good salesmen."

"I guess I'm still a salesman, just an unemployed salesman. A lawyer gets fired he's still a lawyer, an accountants still an accountant, so I guess I'm still a salesman, although apparently not a very good one."

The salesman's little tirade left an awkward pall over the group and all seemed apprehensive about making further comment. Silence prevailed for some time each discombobulated by the situation that had befallen them.

* * *

Then the dapper lawyer offered his cell phone to anyone who might like to use it and then suggested that since they may be a while why not introduce themselves—"As I said my name's Brannon and we've met Mr. Smith here."

The young woman that seemed nervous spoke up, "My name is Carol Reed." She was a pretty woman with auburn hair, smartly dressed, probably about thirty.

Another one of the women said her name was Barker and she was a secretary in the building. Ms. Barker was rather ordinary looking, not unattractive, but she didn't appear to do much for herself in terms of make-up or hair style and was dressed in a plain gray suit. That being noted, she had beautiful blue eyes.

The last woman was the pretty sixty-ish woman with short styled white hair dressed in a blue pants suit. Somehow she projected an air of dignity and self confidence.

The teenage boy was the last to speak, "My name's Bobby and I don't wanna be here."

Introductions completed, other than where did you go to school and where do you live, there was once again fifteen minutes or so of silence; each to his own thoughts about their predicament, accompanied by the drone of piped in music.

* * *

Though there were six of them, the elevator was fairly good sized and they weren't cramped. They were able to turn, lean against a wall and generally move around a bit. The elevator had dark metallic walls but for a mirror at the rear top half. The mirror made things a little uncomfortable trying not to look, yet unavoidably looking at your own and the others' reflections, as if eavesdropping. It was like, I'm not looking at you—I see nothing, but I think you're looking at me. Kinda awkward.

The teenager was looking at Mrs. Reed the edgy woman and he, for whatever reason, blurted out, "Why are your eyes so red? It look like you've been crying."

The lawyer sighed, "Wait a minute young man, I don't believe the young lady has to explain anything to you." He then turned to Mrs. Reid, "Please ignore him."

"That's all right, I don't care," she said, "everybody who knows me, or sees me for that matter, will soon see why I'm upset—why I've been crying. An hour ago I learned that I'm PREGNANT and I don't want to be pregnant—get it?"

That outburst caused another uncomfortable stirring among the elevator passengers. Six people and two already had impulsively shared something that was really no one else's business; first the fired salesman and now the pregnant women. Was this an elevator from hell?

The white haired lady worked her way to the woman's side, and softly said, "Now honey you're going to change your mind about that. Why I have a son and a daughter and three grandchildren. I lost my husband a year ago and I'll tell you I couldn't have made it without my family there for support. It scares me to even think about not having been able to watch and be a part of my children and my grandchildren growing up. I needed them, and they needed me. I cherished the good times and learned from the bad times. I can look at my son and see his father—the dimple in his chin, the little bald spot beginning on the back of his head. No, I wouldn't trade my family for eternal life at the feet of Jesus Christ himself. Mrs. Reed, your doctor didn't just tell you this morning that you were pregnant, rather what he told you makes you the most fortunate among us."

The pregnant passenger responded, "I guess I'll have to think about that."

"You just do that honey."

The lawyer, attempting without success to address only the same two women, said, "I have a wife and two children and I'm awfully proud of them. My wife is what I guess you'd call a community activist. My boy is a senior in high school, gets good grades; good enough that he's had scholarship offers from three different colleges. And, he's a good soccer player—they tell me. My daughter's a high school freshman, doing well and she's as pretty as she can be—like her mother. But, I do wonder sometimes if I've been a good enough father. I've had to work long and hard to become managing partner of our firm and maybe sometimes to the detriment of my wife and kids. I could have done better. Why am I going on like this—forgive me."

The salesman had overheard most of the conversation, "Pa'leez, enough morality philosophy—man, woman, child, makes no difference it's a dog eat dog world out there and the sooner in life one learns that the better off they'll be."

The secretary joined in, "My-my, you're a cynical character aren't you? You know I've seen you around the building for years and I don't ever remember seeing you smile. In fact, I think I've nodded a good-morning to you now and again when we've come face to face and I don't think I ever even got an acknowledgment from you. You need to get a life."

The teenager spoke up, "Hey people, lighten up will ya."

The salesman chimed in, "The kid's right—let's just wait this out in peace and quiet," and with that the group again fell into a period of prolonged silence, except some comments about a recent movie, a new restaurant, the weather.

* * *

Finally, the widow couldn't resist addressing the sales-man's attitudinal problem and broke the silence, "You know Mr. Smith you're really a very pleasant looking fellow. I hope you'll excuse me, but maybe you're in the wrong line of work—maybe sales isn't your forte."

"Funny, I don't recall asking for the opinion of any of you people. Who'da thunk when I got up this morning that before the day was out I'd have the good fortune to receive counsel from a gang of amateur psychologists. I think I've had an epiphany. My father was in life insurance sales with New York Life and made the Million Dollar Round Table fifteen years in a row—taught sales and even wrote a book about sales."

"Well," responded the widow, "sometimes when the acorn falls from the tree the squirrel kicks it into the next county."

The widow wasn't letting go, "The Wright brothers sold and repaired bicycles before they decided to go out and try to build an airplane."

"Yea," the salesman responded, "and Hitler hung wallpaper before he decided to go out and become a dictator and look what happened to him."

That exchange called for a little pause in the conversation, and maybe a little re-adjusting of body parts, clothing, and a sly glance in the mirror. The air-conditioning was still functioning, but nonetheless with six people in close quarters, it seemed to be getting a little stuffy.

* * *

The woman with child seemed to have settled down. She was thinking (*Bob will be happy. He's always wanted children, while I've always managed to skirt the issue. But, I've always enjoyed my personal freedom and a baby will certainly tie me down. There goes some travel plans. In terms of a lifetime though maybe the lady's right, would I get to be fifty and think, my God I'm never going to have a baby? I just don't know*)

The phone rang—the salesman said, "Tell'em to turn off the darn music, I feel like I'm sitting in the string section of the London Symphony."

The lawyer answered and was told the elevator service man was there working on the problem and it shouldn't be too long 'til they'd be moving.

The conversation seemed to be on hold, perhaps because things got a little personal and candid for six people that were essentially strangers. Maybe the forced intimacy subliminally drew them out. The clock continued moving forward.

* * *

The lawyer was thinking (*Why don't I have the same feelings the widow has? I love my wife and kids. I wonder, though, when I last told them that. Betty has always supported me as my career has moved along and she sure seemed happy looking after Ben and Beth. She lives in a beautiful home in a gated community, and pretty much has had a free hand in buying things for herself and the home. I've always told her on her birthday and Christmas to go out and buy whatever she wanted for herself. On the other hand I guess I haven't been too good about surprising her with a gift, flowers, or a dinner out. Maybe I could do better. Maybe I should do better*).

The secretary turned to the distressed salesman, "Really, have you ever thought about another line of work? Sales is probably the toughest line of work there is. Think about it—rejection, rejection, rejection. The high of making a sale must be fleeting. I don't know how anybody does it—it's depressing."

"That may be true," responded the salesman, "but remember—nothin' happens 'til somebody sells something—that's what my father always said."

The secretary thought (*Listen to me, my life hasn't exactly been a party. Why doesn't it bother me? Because I don't expect much that's why. I take care of myself, have friends, and the bottom line is I'm reasonably happy, though I could use a man in my life*).

She asked the salesman, "Are you married?"

"No family."

The widow commented, "My husband made a mid-life career change. He was I guess what you'd call middle management at G.E., and he up and quit, went back to college, got his Masters, Ph.D., and began teaching at a local college. The money was less, but he made a wonderful professor and he was never happier, and consequently neither was I."

The secretary then said, "See, no one ever has to feel they're stuck in their job. Maybe I ought to think about that myself."

The salesman did recall (*Uncle Tom has often told me there's a place for me at his jewelry engraving operation and that one day somebody's going to have to take over. The initial pay wouldn't be great, but heck it's not so great now. I'm going to have to give this some serious thought. Sales has sure proven difficult for me. Maybe it is time for a change. Would Dad be very disappointed?*)

The expectant mother took her turn, "Here you people are talking about jobs, career changes, and so forth, how would you like to be thirty and looking at being stuck at home for the next fifteen or twenty years?"

The secretary had heard enough. "Regrettably, that's an option I've never been able to consider, but I can tell you this, if I had had the opportunity to give birth, nurture a child, teach a child, play with a child, be part of watching a child progress from adolescence to adulthood, I would have embraced the opportunity. What I have for you Mrs. Reed is not empathy, but envy."

"Amen," said the widow lady.

The teenager spoke up, "Is this the kind of crapola I have to look forward to? I coulda stayed home and watched the soaps with my girlfriend if I wanted to listen to this kinda stuff."

The widow responded, "Your time will come kiddo."

"Later rather than sooner I hope."

The lawyer said, "We've been in here almost two hours

now. We should be getting out soon."

"I think I'll sue," said the salesman—"pain, suffering, loss of consortium, wanna represent me?"

"I think I'll pass."

The salesman then, "There's six of us—we could make it a class action suit and you'd get, what? A third of any settlement?"

"Still think I'll pass."

"Just joshing you counselor."

Then silence except for some—when's it going to rain? Wasn't it a hot summer? and like innocuous prattle that prevailed for the next half hour.

* * *

The lawyer spoke up, "Are you OK Mrs. Reed? I could fold up my suit coat and you could sit down on the floor a bit."

"No, I'm fine, thank you."

Then to the widow, "How about you?"

"No, but thank you for your thoughtfulness."

Then another period of silence, each to his own thoughts and by this time each unavoidably profiling fellow captives.

* * *

The widow broke the silence, "Well, I'm sure going to have something to tell my family about. This doesn't happen to everybody."

"No," said the salesman, "Aren't we lucky?"

The secretary reacted, "Know what? Maybe you are lucky. I'll bet it's been a while since you've had such a candid conversation and remember—you started it."

"A while? How about never. But, on the other hand maybe it's an encounter I should have had before this and

111

you're right, I started it."

The teenager had found himself a place to sit on the floor. "I'll bet my girlfriend has gone home." Then looking at the lawyer, "Did you know your hair is kinda orangey on the sides?

"I'll bet she's still here," said the widow.

Just as the salesman was saying, "You know we're pushing three hours," there was a power hum, a surge, and the elevator started to move downward.

"Hallelujah," said the salesman.

"Thank God," the secretary echoed.

All let out a collective sigh of relief.

The doors opened at the lobby landing and the men and boy held back as the women quickly exited the elevator.

There was a cluster of people—building manager, elevator service people and the curious—standing in the lobby at the elevator.

The widow turned to those exiting and said, "This is going to sound weird, but I'm glad I met every one of you and wish each a happy life." She moved to Mrs. Reed and softly said to her, "I promise you, you WILL love that baby and have a happy life."

Mrs. Reed, without even a thought, embraced the widow, "I know I will, thank you so much." After a moment they broke their embrace and moved towards the building exit.

The teenager's girlfriend, also in jeans, sweatshirt, cap on backwards, with straight black hair to her backside had waited for him and they were holding hands as they exited the building.

The secretary moved to the salesman's side and said, "I have no idea why I'm asking this, but would you like to get a cup of coffee? I think perhaps we both still have a lot we could share with one another."

"Would you do that? I'd like that. You know your eyes are a beautiful blue," said the salesman, as they moved towards the coffee shop.

The lawyer, stepped from the elevator, pulled his cell phone from inside his suit coat and punched in a number—

"Miss Turner I think I have a four o'clock with someone from the mayor's office—please call and re-schedule that meeting—my son has a soccer game this afternoon."

END

Charlie's Letter

It had been a dreary overcast morning, but then around noon the sun suddenly burst brightly through the clouds just as the coffin was being lowered into the ground. Dad would have liked that, and for that matter I wouldn't be surprised if he had had a hand in selling the "all mighty" on arranging this moving moment. It would be just like him. The only thing missing was a hallelujah chorus. When the casket hit its final resting place, I was the first to approach the grave, bend down and take a handful of dirt, and drop it in the grave. Dad's younger brother, Uncle Joe, followed my lead, followed by two of my cousins and other family and friends, that is, those who weren't self-conscious about this ritual or simply didn't want to dirty their hands. I shook a few hands, nodded my good-bye's to others, and turned from the burial site and walked towards my rental car intending to drive immediately from Muncie back to the airport in Indianapolis and fly home to Chicago. I'd been through a similar ordeal just six months before when we buried my mother, and now I had to get on with my life minus my mother and father, both of whom I loved dearly, and would miss terribly. Unfortunately my mother went unexpectedly and she and I didn't have an opportunity to say our good-byes. The dreaded phone call, home to be with Dad through the funeral, and back to Chicago. In my dad's case he had pancreatic cancer which is almost always rather fast developing and lethal, but did allow us the time for a visit to express our farewells.

I was an only child and had been away from home for over twenty-five years Dad had wanted me to go into the Chevy dealership with him, but I had my mind set on the law, persisted, went to Ball State there in Muncie and then on to Indiana University for my law degree and was now a partner with a firm in Chicago. The dealership had been started by my mother's father and when mom and dad were married, though my father resisted, he ultimately acquiesced and joined the dealership. It evolved that it was the best thing that ever happened to the dealership as dad was a natural salesman and richly enhanced the business.

As near as I could discern Mom and Dad had had a good

marriage. They always appeared affectionate towards one another, had an active social life, were community activists, and were good practicing Republican Presbyterians.

Anyway, I did make it to Dad's hospital bedside before he died and as I held his hand he asked about my law practice, "Good," was I ever going to get married, "Don't know," passed along that the hospital was trying to poison him as the food was terrible and he suspected that the head floor nurse had a crush on him.

The light patter completed he then squeezed my hand and quite seriously said, "There's something you probably ought to know about before I move on to the other side. Your mother probably wouldn't approve, and I may have to answer to her in the hereafter, but here goes," and then he went on—and what follows are his own words.

"As you know I was born and raised in Philadelphia the son of a fireman and a school teacher. Had the one brother. Soon after I graduated from high school in 1950, uncertain as to what I wanted to do, I made maybe not too bright a decision and joined the army, was sent to Fort Leonard Wood out in the Missouri boonies, and before you could say General McArthur, I was part of the 7th Infantry Division on my way to Korea. I wasn't there long before in a bitterly cold late November I found myself, along with about 20,000 other men from the U.N. forces, surrounded by about 200,000 Chinese, up around the Chosin Reservoir. At the same time the 8th Army was getting their ass kicked over along the Chongchon River. The Chinese weren't supposed to be in this war, or Police Action, but there they were—McArthur blew it—there WE were. Anyway, we were overwhelmed and totally disorganized, when word filtered down through the fractured command that we were to try and make our way to the port city of Hungnam for evacuation.

"I saw a hell of a lot of Chinese during that battle. If you didn't see it you wouldn't believe the way they swarmed up and down those hills in white snow-blending uniforms screaming and blowing trumpets like wild men, day or night.

"It was about five o'clock on a bitterly cold and gray afternoon and as ordered I was looking for a way out when I spotted what looked like an clear alley to the rear, didn't see any of my buddies, so I just ran like hell towards the presumed opening when I suddenly tripped over a downed soldier, my M1 flew through the air and I tumbled to the hard frozen ground. Dazed, I heard a guttural groan coming from the downed man and crawled toward him. I could quickly see there was no helping him as his mid-section was a bloody mess. He was gurgling and blood was trickling down the side of his mouth freezing before it hit the ground. His eyes were open but vacant. He apparently sensed my presence and arm flailing found my arm and grasped my wrist vise-like. He was trying to say something, but even leaning into him, my ear to his mouth, I couldn't make anything out. Straining he then managed to raise an arm and slide a hand in between the buttons of his overcoat, moved his hand around a bit, and came out with an envelope which he pressed into my hand. He nodded his head a couple times and then his head tilted lifelessly to the side and he was gone. I closed his eyes and without even thinking I tucked the envelope into one of my inside coat pockets, looked around for any action, located my M 1, and resumed my run to the rear hoping to escape the carnage.

"I re-connected with some other guys from A Company and ultimately we did make our way to the port city of Hungnam for evacuation which we managed to do in early December, lucky to be alive aboard ship. My mind had been too jumbled to give any thought to my encounter with the dying man on the battlefield. But as things returned to relative normalcy the incident came to mind and I recalled that he had handed me an envelope which should be somewhere among my personal effects. I went through my belongings and sure enough retrieved it from an inside coat pocket. It was a manila colored envelope and in view of the circumstances very lightly smudged. It was addressed to an Elizabeth Trexler, Muncie, Indiana. There was a void between the name and the city with the street addresses apparently to be filled in later; must not have had it at ready when he wrote the letter. The return address just had, PFC Charles Murphy, Somewhere, Korea; Charles had a sense of humor. The letter was sealed and presumably personal between a man and his sweetheart. Respecting Murphy's privacy, I didn't feel I should open it, and not knowing what else to do just put it in my pocket to think about later.

"Later came when I was shipped home in the summer of '52 and discharged—army life over. I held on to the letter perplexed as to what to do with it. I still hadn't opened it; it just wouldn't seem right. I suppose I could have, and maybe should have, tried to run down the street address for an Elizabeth Trexler in Muncie, but I just never did.

"I was back in Philly, visited family, thought about college, but longing for pocket money, found a job selling pots and pans to department stores. I was living with my folks and after being home about a year I had been advanced to a district sales manager position. My boss, the vice-president of sales, always told people I could sell pots and pans to a quadruple amputee. All this time the unopened envelope lay sealed in my top dresser drawer.

"Then after a couple years with the company I was asked to organize a demonstration booth for a kitchen-goods show to be held in Indianapolis. I prepared the necessary, lined up a couple good men to go along, and journeyed to Indianapolis. Before I left Philly I checked my Rand & McNally and found that Muncie was only about sixty miles from Indianapolis. By impulse I took the letter from my dresser drawer and put it in my suitcase.

"The trade show was to run four days. On the second day, comfortable with my sales crew and thinking on it most of a night, I decided to rent a car and drive up to Muncie the next morning and attempt to deliver the overdue letter.

"The next morning, apprehensive, I drove up to Muncie and as Elizabeth had an unusual last name, Trexler, I didn't think I'd have too much trouble running her down. Arriving in

Muncie, I stopped at a filling station and checked a phone book for any Trexlers, and as I suspected there were only two listings, probably related, and I noted the addresses. I wasn't sure if I should call or just stop by. If I, in fact, found Elizabeth I thought it might be, in view of my mission, best to make it face to face rather than a cold phone call and that's what I decided to do. I asked the filling station attendant for street directions and he obliged. I drove the twenty or so blocks to the first address and, on a tree-lined street, pulled up in front of a very nice Tudor-style home. I sat in the car a few minutes trying to sort out what I was going to do and say. I had a strange and painful story to tell. How much of the actual event did I really want to share. Where had I been over these many months. I had no good feelings about any of this, but decided to bull ahead. I retrieved the letter from the glove compartment, slipped it into my coat pocket, exited the car and walked up the flagstone walk to the front door. I rang the doorbell, or chime actually, my stomach tensed, and a woman in a black and white dress, uniform-like, opened the door and quite pleasantly asked my business. I asked her if Elizabeth Trexler lived there and if so was she home. She responded yes, Elizabeth was the homeowners daughter, she was home, and inquired as to who was calling. I told her Bill Andrews and that my visit related to a Charles Murphy. She said, "one moment," and leaving me standing on the front stoop, went back inside and a couple of minutes later a young woman, who was Ava Gardner beautiful, appeared in the doorway; dressed in simple blue-jeans and a blue oxford-cloth shirt, left me momentarily breathless. She was absolutely gorgeous. I introduced myself and she said she was Elizabeth Trexler, asked if I had known Charles, and I could only nod yes which prompted her to ask me in. We settled in a spacious living room where the décor and furnishings were a step or two above what I was accustomed to. After exchanging pleasantries I took a deep breath and carefully proceeded to tell her, as delicately as I could, about my encounter with the dying Charles Murphy. I handed her the letter which she tightly clasped in her hands, said she'd read it momentarily, and went on to explain, that yes, Charles had been her fiance, that they had been high school sweethearts, she the cheerleader and he the star quarterback, and her eyes misted as she went on that they were to be married upon his return from Korea. I was somewhat evasive as to why I was so long in attempting to find her, but she didn't seem to be particularly upset about that and didn't pursue the point. She asked if I could sit still for a few minutes while she got us a soft drink and excused herself. It was maybe five to ten minutes before she returned, noticeably red-eyed, but composed. She had apparently read the letter. She said it was about noon so why didn't I stay for lunch, which I was happy to do. That afternoon I didn't drive back to Indianapolis, but rather she and I found much we seemed to enjoy sharing and the afternoon stretched into our having dinner that evening. We talked about music, jazz and classical, Steinbeck and Kerouc, and movies we especially liked. It may sound Barbara Cartland-like, but there was a chemistry, a drawing together, or at least I felt that way, and, yes, I think she felt the same way.

"After touching base with my guys in Indianapolis I spent the night at a hotel there in Muncie. Before leaving town the next morning I called her to say good-bye and asked her if I was ever back in the area would it be OK to call on her—she said she'd like that. I drove back to Indianapolis that morning closer to the clouds than the highway.

"Well, you know where this is going. I courted your mother long distance between Philadelphia and Muncie for several months, while emotionally the distance became shorter and shorter. I asked her to marry me which she agreed to do with the open end as to where we were going to live. I had advanced nicely at the kitchen-wares company, but she really wanted to stay in Muncie. Your grandfather offered me a spot at the dealership which I resisted, but your mother was quite persuasive and in any event if that was a condition to her marrying me, it was a moot question.

"So, we were married in June, honeymooned in Niagara Falls, returned to Muncie where I went to work at the dealership and eleven months later you were born. I think you'd agree we were a very happy family. Things went well at the dealership and over the first five years I was there we doubled our volume. Life was good.

"Now, to go full circle with this story we must come back to Charles Murphy. I made it a point to meet his parents here in Muncie. They were very gracious and gave your mother and me their blessing in marriage. Let's remember that you and I are here today, my telling this story, only because I stumbled across the dying Charles Murphy on that battlefield in Korea in 1950. The "what ifs" are mind-boggling. War in Korea—the Chinese on the attack—our forces in retreat— the pure chance direction I took in trying to escape that murderous quagmire—pots and pans—a trade show taking me to Indianapolis. And, most astoundingly, the incredible determination and courage of a dying man to retrieve the letter and clasp it into my hand desperate for ultimate delivery to the woman he loved. That was quite a man.

End of story."

Dad said, "Go in the bathroom there and bring me my shaving kit." Which I did, handed it to him, and he unzipped the bag, reached to the bottom and came out with a little leather bound metal flask. "Get a couple glasses from the bathroom." Which I did. "Pour us a couple fingers of Wild Turkey." Which I did.

He handed me one of the glasses, raised his, and I raised mine. We clinked glasses and Dad said, "Here's to the Charlie from that killing field in Korea who isn't here today in body but who's legacy nonetheless lives on through you Charlie who is here today in body—Here, Here, God bless you both, down the hatch."

That was my last visit with Dad: he died six weeks later. I often think about my Mom and Dad, and yes, Charlie Murphy, but for whom, I wouldn't be here today.

END

The Western Military Caper

It seemed like a good idea at the time.

The boys called their club the Eight Balls. There were ten of 'em, but the Ten Balls just didn't seem as apropos as the Eight Balls—didn't sound right. It wasn't a club with defined rules—no charter, by-laws or anything like that— just some fifteen and sixteen year old guys, in 50's suburban St. Louis, who through common interests, naturally gravitated towards one another.

For purposes of this story only six of the Eight Balls were implicated and their profiles are as follows:

As common to most social cliques, leaders commonly simply evolve and the de-facto leader of the Eight Balls was Ray Hansen. Hansen was the go-to guy in determining club activity, e.g. "Whata we gonna do Friday night?" His nickname in the group was Nails—"eats nails and spits rust." Nails was one of those people who possess that natural affinity to lead while others follow. Now that's not necessarily a good thing, and in fact in the story told herein, his judgment might be considered questionable.

Al Marconi, a/k/a The Duke presumed to be second in command. The guys sometimes called him the dago, which he didn't like, so they backed off and called him the wop instead. He claimed that Al Capone was a cousin, but his compatriots had their doubts about that. Duke carried a tough-guy three-quarter inch lead pipe holstered in his cycle boot (no cycle); he drew it, for example, when the guys would go to a movie and the younger set, from their seats, would murmur, "there's the Duke, there's the Duke," the Duke would reach down, draw the pipe from his boot, wrap it soundly a couple of times on the wooden seat-back— "SHAD'UP!"—and the house would settle down. The Duke was the only member of the gang that smoked—started when he was fourteen—and he was a spitter; a fella had to dance around a bit when standing around chatting with the Duke.

Clark Manson a/k/a Indian was called Indian for a quite conspicuous reason—he sported a Mohawk haircut and he was built like a warrior. He was the silent one in the group with a very easy-going personality—for a redskin.

Benny Coen a/k/a B.C. was their only A student, but he didn't flaunt his superior intellect; he dumbed-down to fit in. Benny had a mild case of Tourette's, as manifested by intermittent "beeps" and simultaneous eyes darting skyward. He was gifted musically and was a good trumpet player.

Denny Hogan a/k/a Dandy was one of those neat-as-a-pin kinda guys—everything in its place—hair perfect, starched Levi's—a guy just wanted to muss his hair and pull out his shirt-tail. He was the center of life for his diminutive divorced mother and his grandmother.

Chris Pappas a/k/a The Greek, with olive-complexion, coal black hair, was a good-lookin' kid. He was super cool wearing a fedora-like Pledgeworth hat—short dome, brim turned up in back—and Threadneedle Street ("Threads") oxblood shoes.

The usual meting place for the Eight Balls was either the Delmar-Trinity Avenue corner in front of Walgreen's or the booths inside at the soda fountain/grill. They'd stand on the corner passing the time of day, dodging the Duke's habitual spitting—"Chevy"—"whata we gonna do?"—"Buick"—"how about some penny-ante poker?"—"Mercury"—"Naw, let's—Ford—shoot some baskets"—"Chevy"—"let's just go in—Packard—and get a coke."

Neither the Walgreen's manager, Mr. Burlmaster, nor the fountain manager, Chuck, particularly liked to see the Eight Balls coming and taking up a couple of booths for a few Cokes. Chuck, a WW Two vet, was a nice enough guy, and quite proud of his title of "fountain manager." He wasn't real bright though—like the time the boys convinced him you had to have a passport to get into Heaven.

"Chuck, do you have to have a passport to get into France?"

"Yea."

"Do you have to have a passport to get into Germany?"

"Yea."

"Now, are you gonna sit there and tell me you have to have a passport to get into France, you have to have a passport to get into Germany, but you don't have to have a passport to get into Heaven?"

"No, no, I guess you would."

"Case closed."

Chuck usually tolerated the boys in good cheer. Mr. Burlmaster, balding fifty-ish five foot two heightened by elevator-shoes to five-six, on the other hand, found the boys a nuisance and unsuccessfully discouraged their patronage. When he came at the boys, with a red face running up and over his bald head, they knew it was time to leave.

Though the Eight Balls may have been described as a gang, they weren't of the menacing variety. The only crooked thing they did was to occasionally stuff napkins bits up the coin return slot in the Walgreen's telephone booth. Duke did carry the lead pipe down his cycle-boot, but never threatened anyone over eight years old. Ray had a switchblade knife, but the spring broke, so he loaded it down with sewing machine oil and with a brisk flick of the wrist the blade would fly out. However, he had to quit packing it as the machine oil left an indelible stain on his pants pockets and his mother raised heck about him ruining his trousers. The only fisticuffs of note were between two of their own, Duke and Dandy, when they got into it over Nicki Collins, but you can't blame 'em for that—she was real cute and enjoyed playing one off the other.

The only time the Eight Balls had a run-in with the police resulted from a night when five of the guys were taking turns climbing up a tree outside Judy Edwards bedroom window when she was having a slumber party and the Duke fell out'a the tree breaking his wrist, screaming, when hitting the ground. Alerted, Mr. Edwards called the police on 'em and the cops hauled them, except Indian, who managed to slip away, to the police station, sat 'em down on a bench, and had a menacing detective stare at them for a hour or so before turning them loose with a warning. "Next time you guys could be looking at jail time."

Well, there was the time four of the Eight Balls followed the dog-catcher wagon around town 'til the dog-catcher stopped the truck and got out to chase down a stray. The boys managed to release all the previously captured dogs. Unfortunately, somebody recognized one of the Eight Balls, reported him to Animal Control, and a couple of the guys got in a little trouble over that.

But, the point is, none of the Eight Balls ever made MOST WANTED.

In 1950 the Eight Balls experienced their first informal resignation from the club when Denny Hogan's mother apparently came to the dubious conclusion that her darling boy would be better influenced in a military environment, rather than an Eight Ball environment. So, one fall it was off-you-go to Western Military Academy up the Mississippi in Alton Illinois just north of St. Louis. Denny had resisted, but mother prevailed. The boys ceremoniously gifted Denny Ray's moderately rusty Red Ryder B-B Gun, and with proper ceremony, bade him a fond farewell.

Denny came home on furlough that first Christmas and he had the audacity to sport his military uniform when meeting up with the Eight Balls. He wore a gray uniform, brass buttons, black stripe down the trousers, black tie, black epaulet's, spit shinny black shoes, and military style brimmed cap. The Eight Balls rode Denny unmercifully about being a toy soldier, but Dandy Denny quite readily deflected any attempt at mockery; he was quite pleased with himself.

Before returning to Western, after the Christmas break, Denny gave Ray his address and asked that he drop him a line now and again regarding the club activities and provide updates on the comings and goings of Nicki Collins. Ray, as the titular head of the Eight Balls, told Denny he'd do his best to accommodate.

One very pleasant spring evening five of the fore-mentioned Eight Balls found themselves at a loss as to what to do that night. They'd seen the movies at both the Varsity and the Tivoli. There were no known girlfriends having a slumber party. Ray had the car that night and they had already cruised the drive-in restaurants looking for girls on a similar mission. Then, somehow in the course of the deliberations, Denny Hogan came up in the conversation—"Wonder what old Denny's up to?"—"Sure miss the guy"—Then B.C. said, "Why don't we drive up and see the guy?"

Chris said, "It'd take us forty-five minutes or so just to drive up there."

"Beep!"

The Indian responded, "So what."

The Duke, "How would we find him?"

Ray remembered, "I've got his location right here in my wallet—building number, room number, the whole works."

B.C. said, "He'd be in bed by this time."

The Indian responded, "So what."

"Beep!"

"Whata we going to do Ray?" asked Chris.

The boys looked to Ray as he pondered for a few fleeting seconds—"It's a GO!"

It did take about forty-five minutes to drive up and over the Mississippi into Alton. Western Military was not far from the downtown and a couple of the guys, having been there before, knew their way around, and they were pulling up to the campus area in just a few minutes.

"There's the sign:"

Western Military Academy
Estab. 1895

Ray said, "We'll park just down the street a little where we'll be a little less conspicuous; they gotta have night watchmen."

Clark said, "As I recall there are three or four dorms right in a row about central campus."

Ray, having retrieved Denny's address, said, "He's in E Barracks, 206—I assume that means the second floor. OK guys we'll head straight for that school sign, get our bearings, and go from there. Ready? Now be quiet. B.C. watch the beeping. Let's go."

They exited the car and crept towards the school sign,

passing under a brick archway and onto school grounds, hesitated, and Clark softly said, "There, over there, see that row of three-story buildings? I'm sure those are the barracks."

The moon was just bright enough that they could see adequately.

Ray said, "OK, let's go—quietly now."

They approached the first old brick building—D Barracks over the front door.

"Got to be the next building," said Ray—and it was.

The boys slipped up the few concrete steps to E Barracks and Ray tried the door latch—open.

One by one they entered the barracks and gathered in a cluster in the first floor front foyer. As Denny's room number was 206 they had surmised he was on the second floor. There were soft night lights in the hall and the boys crept up the center hall steps to the second floor and arbitrarily took a right. The first door was 204—close—two doors further—206.

Ray put a finger to his lips—"quiet"—slowly turned the doorknob—opened the door a bit and slipped a hand into the room feeling the wall for a light-switch—found it—motioned, "all set," to his companions—flipped the light-switch—and the five Eight Balls burst through the door—"SURPRISE!"

From a lower bunk, "JESUS CHRIST ALMIGHTY!" It was Denny instantly on his feet. "Are you guys NUTS! Be quiet, quiet."

The room was about 12by15 with double-decker bunk beds, a couple dressers, two desks with straight-back wooden chairs—militarily Spartan. The upper bunk held a freckled-face red-headed kid, bug-eyed, who was knotted up cowering in a corner of his bunk. Both cadets were in white boxer shorts and tee-shirts.

"Just thought we'd stop by see ya old buddy."

"How's military life?"

"Beep."

Denny kept mumbling, "You guys are nuts, you guys are

nuts—you're gonna get me kicked outta here."

"You are glad to see us aren't you general?"

"Yea, we drove all the way up here just to see you."

Denny calmed down a bit, "What's going on at home? Is Nicki seeing anybody?"

"Naw."

Denny said, "That's Archie up there in the top bunk—he's from Chicago."

"Hi Archie."

No response—just that, God help me look.

Denny exclaimed, "Where's the beer? How come you didn't bring me a beer?"

"No money. Who's that guy in the picture on the wall?"

"That's Paul Tibbets the guy that dropped the bomb on Hiroshima—he went here."

"No shit."

About three or four minutes into their arriving, B.C. noticed a bugle sitting on one of the desks, and being a brass man, he queried, "Who's bugle?"

"That's Archie's," replied Denny, "Now put it down."

Did B.C. put the bugle down? NO, he didn't put it down, and using rather poor judgment, raised the bugle to his lips, took a deep breath.

"NO!"

And blew revelry, without benefit of accustomed trumpet valves, but nonetheless blasted a passable report in the 12by15 room that assaulted the ear drums.

Denny shouted, "JESUS CHRIST, JESUS CHRIST!"

Archie pulled his covers over his head trembling.

The boys, all five, tried to bolt through the door at the same time, arms and legs flailing, with some popping through, and others tumbling to the floor blocking the way out.

All the time Denny, "JESUS CHRIST, JESUS CHRIST—JUDAS PRIEST!"

The Eight Balls ran down the hall, down the steps, bursting through the front door running and stumbling as in a stampede.

Hitting the outside some were disoriented as to where the car was parked. Now there were a couple other people running around helter-skelter with flashlights—yes, night watchmen.

Duke ran smack-bam into a tree—bloodying his nose.

Chris, trying to escape, tangled with a fence, or something, and ripped his shirt up the backside.

Ray, running in the dark, ran directly, face first, into what was apparently a tennis court fence—BOING!—and was catapulted directly to his backside.

The night watchmen were running and yelling, "HALT', HALT."

Lights in the barracks were popping on in mass.

Somehow, by no small miracle, all five made it to and in the car. Ray fumbled for his keys, got the car started, peeled rubber, as they sped away from Western Military and the pursuing night watchmen.

Ray wasted no time driving the several blocks back to downtown Alton, the Mississippi bridge, and back over into Missouri. They were completely out of breath, panting, and incredulous as to the turn of events.

Ray was the first to speak, "Seemed like a good idea at the time," and with that they all busted out laughing and back slapping.

"B.C. you crazy son'bitch."

"Surprised hell outta Denny didn't we."

"NO SHIT!"

"I'll bet Archie's still on his bunk rolled up into a ball."

"HAR, HAR, de'HAR, HAR"

So the Eight Balls all told, and retold, their version of the raid, each trying to top the other, and each laughing his misguided head off.

They were nearing home base when Indian suggested they follow their customary routine and stop at the CURTESY DINER for a Coke or coffee before calling it a night, which they all agreed to.

Arriving at the white metal clad diner and entering was the first time since the raid the boys had been subjected to bright lights.

"Holy shit," look at Ray's face.

They all turned to Ray, who reacted, "What's the matter?"

What the matter was, was that as a consequence of colliding with the tennis court fence face-first he had little red circles all over his face, cheeks, forehead, and a bullseye around his nose.

"Look at yourself in the mirror—you're a mess."

Ray looked, "OH MY GOD!"

"Beep."

Duke turned to Earl the counterman, "Earl get me a dish rag and some ice cubes."

Duke wrapped some ice cubes in the dish rag, handed it to Ray, "Keep dabbing at your face; that oughta help."

Ray followed Duke's counsel, "Thanks."

There were cuts, bruises, serious grass stains, and torn clothing among the others, but thankfully no broken bones or teeth knocked out.

The Duke did bruise his ankle a bit as a consequence of running wearing a cycle boot with the lead pipe stuffed down inside.

The Indian was the only one to escape totally unscathed as he was cable of moving swiftly and silently—not a scratch on him.

After an half hour or so of settling down the boys were ready to call it a night, exited CURTESY, and climbed back into Ray's car to be dropped off at home one by one.

Ray finally arrived home about 1:30, got the door key from under the front porch flower pot, went in and straight up to his bedroom. He made his evening concluding trip to the bathroom and with some reluctance checked his face in the mirror. The red circles were still there, but fading. The ice-pack had apparently helped.

As Ray drifted off to sleep, he couldn't but smile—"what a night."

* * *

Ray slept 'til about nine on Sunday morning and to please his mom and dad was up in time to go to Sunday School at First Pres. His dad asked what he had done the night before.

"Oh, just hung around with the guys."

Ray's mom said it looked like he had some kind of red marks on his face.

"Just pimples I guess."

"In ringlets?"

All and all it was a quiet Sunday.

* * *

Ray got home from school about 4 o'clock on Monday. He was barely through the door when his mother, walking from the kitchen, said, "Talk to you for a minute. I got a call this morning from the Alton Illinois Police Department, a sergeant Ryan; seems our car was spotted in Alton Saturday night and the passengers in the car had apparently caused a big ruckus at Western Military Academy. A night watchman had noted the out of place Missouri tag, took down the number, and while the ruckus was underway he called the police who consequently set up a road-block at the bridge, but the mischievous car managed to slip through before the police were set up. He went on to say they have the license number, a description of the car, and if the car should ever be spotted in Alton again the driver and any passengers would be detained and possibly be looking at charges for illegal trespassing, vandalism and malicious mischief. So, do you want to tell me about it?"

"Well Mom, you see Denny Hogan…."

END

EPILOGUE

Denny Hogan a/k/a Dandy didn't graduate from Western Military. It had nothing to do with the raid; he just got some deportment demerits and dorm restrictions for that. (Actually the only raid casualty was Archie who consequently had trouble sleeping at night. Ultimately his parents had him moved from E Barracks 206 to A Barracks 100.) With Denny, due to some apparent re-occurrence of family turmoil, after a couple of years at Western, he went to live with his father in Southern California, never to be heard from again.

Al Marconi a/k/a The Duke didn't graduate from high school. He joined the Navy after his junior year and while home on his first leave married a local girl. In the Post Dispatch wedding announcement Al had himself described as "night fighter pilot." He may have served on an aircraft carrier, but the closest he ever got to an airplane was for re-fueling. After the navy Al got his high school equivalency and was working in sales for G.E. in California, with his second, or maybe third, wife. He died of lung cancer while still in his forty's.

Clark Manson a/k/a The Indian never married and had a successful career as a loan officer for a suburban St. Louis bank. As of this writing he is still living in the house to which he was brought home from the hospital as a baby some seventy years ago.

Benny Coen a/k/a B.C. wasn't much on the bugle but his trumpet playing got him a gig on the road for a time with Wayne King the *"Waltz King."* Medical advances ultimately pretty much controlled the Tourette's. He went on to have a very successful career in the manufacturing field and is now retired and living in St. Louis.

Chris Pappas a/k/a The Greek for many years owned and

operated a very successful mid-town St. Louis bar and grill as well as having lucrative real estate investments. He waited 'til his fifty's to get married and is now retired and playing golf in and around suburban St. Louis.

Ray Hansen a/k/a/ Nails enjoyed success in the insurance business in Ohio, where he also held various leadership positions in community and civic organizations. He is now retired and living somewhere in the Southeast.

The Western Military Academy, along with many other military prep schools, ultimately lost its luster, and with the additional negative impact of the war in Vietnam, played taps for the final time in 1971.

Lessons Learned

Paul Stover always tried to get to the annual Blue Coats dinner held at the country club. Not the least of reasons, it was one of the few remaining stag events in the entire U.S. of A. The Blue Coats annual dues was a hundred dollars which went to an education fund for the children of police officers killed or disabled in the line of duty—a good cause. There must have been a couple hundred Blue Coats with probably half that number showing up each year for the annual dinner. The dinner usually featured a cash bar and a first rate light buffet dinner. No formal program, rather just an opportunity to get together socially with ones peers and some folks from law enforcement.

Paul had had a busy and exasperating day—busy at the office trying to wrap up a bid for replacing the floor of a local high school gymnasium and exasperating, because due to the economic slowdown, he had to let one of his salesmen go. He hated letting Bill go because he was the superior salesman, and to make it worse it was a clear case of discrimination. The other two guys had families and Bill didn't—he was single—lousy deal. Paul did give him three months severance which he hoped would lessen the sting.

Tall Oaks Country Club, though old and stodgy, was the "who's who" club in the community, which would include Paul Stover. Maybe because he was upset about his day, or the slow down in business in general, at dinner he probably had a martini, or two, more than his usual self-imposed limit of two. Enjoying being with friends, talking sports and politics, made him feel better, and what the hell, he was entitled to a good time now and again.

Paul got a plate at the food spread and had a few shrimp, some of those little meatballs and franks, some black olives—he loved black olives—and some veggies, which made for his supper for the evening.

After being there an hour or so he thought he was exercising pretty good judgment when he shut down the marts, bade his friends farewell, and exited the club to find his Buick in the parking lot and head for home. It was a beautiful fall evening and he was feeling quite a bit better after a couple of drinks and good cheer with friends. All and all, things were pretty good. He hadn't driven more than a mile or so from the club when a red light began flashing in his rear-view mirror. He pulled to the side of the road so the presumed emergency vehicle could pass, but the flasher simply pulled in front of Paul, slowed, inferring Paul should pull over. Paul thought that curious; he didn't think he'd done anything wrong, but followed directions, pulled over and stopped along side the road, put the car in neutral, and lowered the window. After a bit a police officer got out of his car and walked back towards Paul's car and his open window.

"Good-evening officer," Paul said.

"Good-evening sir. Turn off your ignition. May I see your drivers license please."

"Sure," and Paul retrieved his drivers license from his wallet and handed it to the officer.

"You know Mr. Stover you took a mighty wide turn back there and your driving seems a little erratic. What year is your car?"

"Ah, it's an 07, no 08."

"What color?"

"Ah, Silver."

"Please step out of the car Mr. Stover."

Paul got out of the car and stood along side.

The officer said, "Put your right arm out here in front and bring your hand back and touch the tip of your nose with your index finger."

"OK"—missed by a bit.

"Now while I stand here you walk towards me one foot right in front of the other."

"OK"—not quite.

"Mr. Stover, I'll have to take you in for suspected Driving Under the Influence. We'll leave your car here, you'll go with me to the station, when there you can make a phone call for someone to come and get you and also make arrangements for you to retrieve your car—OK?"

There were really no options. Ironic that he just left a meeting benefiting law enforcement; being stopped so soon thereafter he couldn't help but wonder if he'd been entrapped. On the other hand he had to concede he sure flunked the roadside sobriety tests. All irrelevant—he was being hauled in. "OK."

Paul locked up his car and got in the back seat of the cop car and they traveled the several miles to the police station. Once there and going in the arresting officer turned him over to another uniform to administer a breathalyzer—"Just over."

"Swell," barely pregnant.

They sat Paul down by a phone, he was given a phone book, and he looked up the number of Todd Martin, his attorney, to make arrangements to be picked up. He dialed and got Mrs. Martin and reluctantly explained his situation. She said that was unfortunate, but Todd had attended the same affair and was in no condition to go anywhere, and in particular not to a police station.

However, she said she'd call one of Todd's partners to see about filling in for Todd. Paul thanked her and perhaps dubiously added, "Best regards to Todd," and hung up hopeful he'd soon be outta there.

Then the uniform said, "You'll have to wait in the tank for your pick up," and he led Paul through a couple doors to a room that housed a lone wire cage, probably about twenty by twenty. There were four or five guys in the cage sitting on a wooden bench or standing leaning against the wire cage.

From a burly guy in a tee shirt and jeans, "Hey! When am I getting outta here?"

"Relax and enjoy your leisure time," said the cop—"In here Stover."

The cop closed and locked the door and Paul walked straight to the closest bench and sat down.

He wasn't any more than down when a young slightly built bald-headed guy in a sweat-suit came over, sat down next to Paul, and said, "Whatta they got you for?"

"D.U.I."

"Oh, I've been in for that before."

"Really." (who cares).

"This time they got me good though."

"Oh, really?"

"Yea, they've tagged me a Cereal Killer."

"SERIAL KILLER!"

"Yea, they've been laying for me for some time and now they actually caught me in the act."

Paul scooted a little further down the bench—"Really."

"Yea, they caught me in KROGERS stabbing cereal boxes with a butcher knife."

"DOING WHAT?"

"Stabbing cereal boxes with a butcher knife, and by God I got a dozen or so. Did you know that every box of cereal contains riboflavin and a state funded laboratory in Bosnia found that riboflavin is a cancer agent? So, I see it as my duty to mankind, as long as I can take breath, to go out and kill as many breakfast cereal boxes as humanly possible, but I don't think my efforts are appreciated."

"Yea?" (Great Paul thought, a genuine wacko cereal killer). "I wish you great success; now why don't you move along and share your theory with somebody else?"

"Sure, sure, you think I'm crazy too, you'll be sorry, you'll all be sorry."

Paul noticed a sulking medium-sized guy in a tee-shirt and denim shorts, who looked to be covered with bruises and contusions, sitting opposite and couldn't resist walking over, "Whatta you here for?"

He responded, "They say it's a man's world—that's bullshit!—it's a woman's world. I come home from a hard days work at the shop looking for a brew, maybe a cigar, and some relaxation. No stop-off at a tavern or nothin'. I walk through the door and immediately encounter a bitch from hell. She's been home all day, had several beers, and for who knows why in hell is surly. I try casual small talk, how was your day? and she screams"—

"Whatta you care asshole!"

"And, away we go! One thing led to another and she starts

swinging and throwing stuff at me—a beer bottle, frying pan. I'm ducking and dodging, but not fast enough, and she's scoring some hits. I manage to get to a phone and call 911 and tell 'em I need the police. Inside five minutes two cops come busting through the front door"—

"OK what's goin' on here?"

She screams, "He's been beating me! He's a big bully!"

"Oh yea," says a cop and they knock me to the floor. "Spread eagle buster," as they cuff me, pat me down, pull me to my feet and lead me out the door, as I hear from behind, "That'll learn ya, you big bully!" and I'm thrown into a squad car."

I say, "BUT!"

"Better shut up buddy you're in deep shit already."

Paul said, "Didn't you tell them what actually happened?"

They wouldn't listen, just said, "Sure, sure, we've heard it all before."

Paul could think of nothing else to say—"Your wife needs help."

"Hell look at me! I'm the one that needs help; one a these days she's gonna kill me."

"Hang in there," as Paul moved along to another spot on a bench.

Paul was thinking (Where in the hell is that attorney—wonder who they'll send—shouldn't have had that last martini)

As Paul sat there he heard a, "Phsst, Phsst," and turned to see a little guy wiggling a come-hither finger towards him.

Paul pointed at his chest as if to ask, "Who, me?" and the guy nodded, "Yes."

Paul said,"What the hell, why not, been that kinda night," and moved over to where the guy sat, who then inquired of Paul, "Whatta ya in for?"

"Looks like a D.U.I.—how about you?"

"They got me for trespassing. They caught me sleeping in a bed in PENNY'S when they opened this morning. Made a big fuss. They wanted to charge me with breaking and entering, but there were no signs of forcible entry so they had to settle for trespassing."

"What were you doing sleeping in PENNY'S?"

"Well, a guy's gotta sleep somewhere doesn't he?"

"Point taken."

"Fact is, I didn't sleep all that well, there must have been ten clocks tick-tocking at me all night—TICK-TOCK, TICK-TOCK, drove me nuts."

The guy had his head shaved near bald, wore wire-rim glasses, and looked to be partly oriental—his eyed were kinda squinty; said his name was Raymond.

Raymond then said, "Keep your voice down and come closer. You look like a man of some intelligence, and means, so I'm gonna take a chance and share something with you. I've got an idea on a way to make a lot of money and I could squeeze in a partner."

Paul, couldn't believe his luck and responded, "Oh, pray-tell."

Raymond looked around to make sure no one else was listening and went on, "I envision a business of re-cycling toothbrushes and re-selling them as grout cleaning brushes. Think about it, we'd accumulate them, clean'em up, re-package 'em, and sell'em to LOWES and HOME DEPOT, who'd peddle'em along with the other grout cleaning stuff. I bet they'd both jump at it. We could make a fortune."

Paul couldn't resist, "Why wouldn't people just save their toothbrushes themselves to use later for cleaning grout?"

Raymond had an answer, "They just wouldn't—think about it. You know how you throw away your empty PLANTERS PEANUT cans and then the next time you have to clean a paint brush you think, damn, why didn't I save that peanuts can. People just don't think to save that kinda stuff."

"Well I gotta say, you got a point there Raymond, but tell me how are you going to collect all those toothbrushes?"

Raymond thought for a minute, "Well, you can't leave everything to me; if you're gonna take fifty-percent of the company I oughta at least be able to count on you for somethin', don't ya think?"

Paul, incredulous, responded, "Have you offered this to anyone else?"

"Well, I did talk to my brother-in-law about it, but he's so dumb he thought grout was something you get when your feet swell up—can you believe that?"

"I think that may be gout your brother-in-law was thinking of, Raymond."

"Whatever."

"Sounds interesting though, Raymond. Tell you what, I'll have my people call your people."

Paul wondered (Is it me, the booze, or have I just been deposited in a looney-bin)?

(Paul sat in solitude for a while commiserating with himself—fine mess you got yourself into this time).

There was only a couple remaining people Paul hadn't encountered, so, "What the hell."

He walked over to one of the guy sitting on a bench in the corner, "Hello there."

"Hey," the guy responded.

"Everybody else is sharing their misfortune, whata you doing here?"

The guy stood up and on his feet in full body Paul could see he was clearly a body builder. His neck looked to be about a size twenty-six and his arm muscle's dropping from his cut-off tee shirt bulged grotesquely. He was probably only about five-eight and he resembled a bundle of bricks. He reported, "I was at my girlfriends house—we'd had a few—she insulted me—barely touched her—she called the police on me and here I sit."

"Yea," Paul said, "as my friend over there said—it's a woman's world."

"You got that right."

"What'd your girlfriend say to insult you?"

"I don't wanna talk about it."

"Must have been pretty bad."

"Well, if you really must know," as he grabbed Paul's

arm and pulled him closer, "she said steroids were getting the better of me and that my Johnson was beginning to look like a week old frankfurter supporting two used tea bags. Those were her exact words—bitch!"

Paul choked and sputtered, "Well, well, I guess, I guess, that would make anybody mad."

"Damn right!"

Paul went on, "I'll bet she's sorry she said that—probably just wasn't thinking straight—maybe you oughta give her another chance."

"Maybe—bitch!"

Paul was thinking (I gotta get the hell outa here).

It had been close to two hours and Paul was getting a little anxious. (Where the hell's my attorney? How many drinks did I have? Three I think. This is gonna be embarrassing. Terri's gonna be pissed. Thankfully the kids are away at school.)

It looked like Raymond, the toothbrush entrepreneur, was trying to sell one of the other guys on his scheme—it was the last guy Paul hadn't talked to—but he then walked over to where Paul was sitting.

"Find another prospective partner?" asked Paul.

"Naw, another one that didn't even know what the hell grout was—idiot."

"What's that guy being held for?"

"He's looking at a charge of being a peeping Tom, but he says it aint so. He says he was just taking a short-cut through this yard and playing catch with his cap when he threw his cap too high in the air and it got caught up in a tree. He had to climb the tree to retrieve the cap and it just happened to be outside some woman's bedroom window—he got caught."

"Sounds plausible," Paul said. (Get me outta here).

It must have been two hours since being incarcerated when a Blue finally came through the door, "Who's Stover?"

"I am," quickly responded Paul.

"Your lawyer's here for ya," as he walked over, and

unlocked the door.

Paul exited the tank and didn't even look back, but heard, "Hey, how about me," over his shoulder.

"Yea, me too."

"Keep in touch"—no doubt the toothbrush guy.

Paul followed the officer into the squad room and immediately recognized Art Delaney one of Todd's law partners.

"Hey Paul, over here. You have to sign this receipt for the court summons and we're outta here."

An officer behind a desk held out a clip-board with a paper for Paul to sign and receive a copy. Paul looked quizzically at Delaney who said, "Go ahead and sign, not much of an alternative at this point." Paul signed and hurried out the door.

Art brought his wife with him to the police station and she was waiting in the car and they then drove to where Paul's car was left roadside. Then Art and Paul got in Paul's car for Art to drive Paul home as Art's wife followed. Paul was confident he was fully sober by this time but, that was the arrangement the police agreed to.

Number one attorney's wife, Barb, had tipped off Paul's wife, Terri, as to the evenings events, and even though he knew damn well she'd still be awake, he crept into the house like he was going to get away with something, but she did greet him icily at the second floor landing; about all he got from her was, "You know two's your limit—hope you've learned your lesson."

"Honey, you have no idea...."

* * *

It may not have been fair to society at large, but though he made a court appearance and paid a fine, Paul's connections quietly got him out of the usual remedial driving classes, and from the D.U.I. listings in the newspaper. The D.M.V. was also kept out of the loop. Paul got some breaks as the whole sorry episode was pretty much kept under wraps. He knew he made a mistake and he truly did watch his drinking and driving after that—he wouldn't make that mistake again. However, he wasn't big enough to overlook the suspicion of entrapment and spitefully dropped his membership in the Blue Coats.

Well, nobody's perfect.

END

Heaven—In Time

It was a heck of a snowstorm and the ground, sidewalk, and driveway were covered with a good four inches of the white stuff. It was kinda pretty, but the snow blanketed on the sidewalk and driveway had to go if Marty and family were to remain mobile. So, like it or not, about ten am on a Saturday morning he had to adorn his down LIONS jacket, stocking cap, boots and gloves, de-rack the snow shovel in the garage, and putting shoulder behind the shovel, clear off the darn pretty white snow. Fortunately their small brick bungalow had a companion small sidewalk and driveway. Michigan in late November and this was only act one in what would surely be snows opportunity to offer a long winters program.

It took Marty about an hour of huffing and puffing—and a little swearing—to clear the sidewalk and driveway to the point of once again being usable. He was irritated that Murphy, across the street, was showing off his new snow blower and he hadn't worked in six months. There's just no justice. Just to be on the safe side he sprinkled a little salt on the sidewalk as in these litigious days one can never be too cautious. Just his luck and Steinmetz, that cranky old goat next door, would find a way to slip and fall on Marty's sidewalk, break a leg, and sue for ten million. Marty took a step back and surveyed his work, satisfied, he stomped the snow off his boots, brushed it off his jacket and went back into the garage, shed his winter gear, re-racked the snow shovel, and went inside the house to catch his breath and have a hot cup of coffee, maybe spiked with a shot of Jim Beam. He had an afternoon of TV football to look forward to. Carol, sweet, pretty, and diminutive, already had an un-spiked coffee waiting for him as he sat down at the kitchen table to wind down.

"Marty, you're out of breath—you should have let that Jansen kid shovel the snow. What's a couple dollars?"

"A couple cans of beer."

He had just taken a few sips of coffee when he suddenly felt a sharp pain down his left arm followed immediately by a tightening pain in his chest; he fell from the chair to the floor—groaning and seeming to be semi-conscious.

"MARTY! MARTY!" as Carol dropped to the floor at Marty's side, "MARTY! 911, 911," Carol cried as she ran to the 'phone and dialed.

"911 here—what's your emergency?"

"I need help! need help! my husband's collapsed on the kitchen floor and I can't tell if he's conscious or not—he's not responding."

"Your address ma'am?"

"7235 Colgate."

"All right ma'am, help is on the way—you're very close to our mobile unit—try your best to stay calm. It should just be a few minutes before they'll be there. Do you know how to administer CPR?"

"NO!"

"We'll keep it simple. Right now, kneel at his side, place one hand in the center of his chest and place the other hand on top of that hand—then with your shoulders directly over him push down hard and fast thirty times, a couple seconds between thrusts—then get back with me."

Marty was on his back and as best she was able Carol followed the CPR instructions then went back to the 'phone—"OK, done."

"Now put your ear to his mouth and see if you sense any breath."

Carol bent down, "YES, YES, I do. And I hear a siren."

"Good girl."

"Oh Marty, hang in there sweetheart, help is almost here."

It was only a matter of minutes after Carol frantic call when two EMS men burst through the door, equipment in hand, and immediately began administering first aid.

"He's barely conscious, but breathing ma'am, we'll get him to Emergency pronto," as the two men lifted Marty to a gurney and wheeled him, with resuscitation equipment humming, to and into the emergency vehicle—Carol close behind.

"You'll be OK sweetie," not knowing if he was compre-hending her speaking as he was totally non-responsive—she was in the ambulance, beside him, holding his hand.

The ambulance, siren howling, bolted in and around traffic, winding its way to Emergency. Noon'ish on Saturday so thankfully the traffic was not too bad.

Upon arrival at the hospital the attendants jumped from the ambulance, rolled Marty through the automatic doors, Carol along side, into EMERGENCY, a nurse stopping Carol at the inner door.

The nurse took Carol's arm and led her into a small waiting area—"You wait here hon, we'll get to you as soon as we have some news."

Carol sat, and for the first time in quite a while, she prayed. She felt guilty about that—only acknowledge Him when you need Him. "Pull him through and I'll do better—promise."

In the emergency room Marty had been transferred from a gurney to a treatment table and was hooked up to appropriate beeping and humming life sustaining paraphernalia.

Marty was out of it, but a few minutes in, as if reacting to an arm tug, he suddenly found himself aware of rising from the table and floating upward, yet as he looked down, he saw himself still lying on the table in the clothes he had on when coming in from shoveling the snow. He saw hospital staff around him probing at his lifeless form—a maze of beeping equipment, lights flashing, all around the room. He sensed a continuing rise upward and then he seemed to be entering a tunnel with a beckoning white light to his front. Then he felt a sudden SWOOSH and he was at the end of the tunnel and was looking at a huge black hole. Still floating he traveled through the black holes entrance and again a SWOOSH— and in an instant he remarkably found himself standing on a green grassy knoll under a spacious blue, yet rainy, sky.

"WHAT's goin' on?"

Then Marty heard an, "Over here."

He looked to his right and saw a man, dressed in what looked like a blue Mao outfit, motioning Marty over—"Over here."

Marty, now totally discombobulated, unwittingly fol-lowed instructions and walked towards the somewhat elderly man. Now he saw the man was standing, out of the rain, under what was a canopy-like structure housing a mish-mash of canvas directors chairs. He could also see there were some other men and women, some in the blue Mao outfits, milling around. As Marty approached the gentleman held out his hand, Marty reciprocated, and as the man clasped Marty's hand he quite warmly said, "Welcome to Heaven."

"WHAT," exclaimed Marty, "GET OUTTA HERE!"

"Heaven—My name's Jacob, I'm your acclimator, and hope to be your friend. Please try and be calm. Your initial reaction is not unlike most others and please trust me when I say, more readily than you may think, you'll accept the idea. My purpose here is to assure you that those you left behind, though grieving, with prayer, will manage to get through the ordeal of facing the death of a loved one. Always remember—life goes on. What we need to do is to sit down and via a crash course I'll tell you pretty much what to expect while here and answer any questions you may have. So, shall we sit, have a cup of tea, and talk."

As he sat Marty responded, "For starters—exactly where am I—besides just being in Heaven? for which, incidentally, I am of course grateful. That is, if I'm dead and gotta be somewhere."

"Well," Jacob said, "for starters, as to where are you, I'm sure within the past several years you've read and heard scientists on earth talk about finding 'black holes' in the universe."

"Yeah."

"Well, those 'black holes' are actually the entrance-ways to Heaven and once deeply through the 'black holes' one arrives at what you see here—an infinite land of green and blue—we've called Heaven."

"I can't believe it; I was just shoveling my sidewalk only, what, fifteen, twenty, minutes ago? Carol was right—I should have let that Jansen kid shovel the snow. Why me?"

"Pure chance, my boy."

"Does everyone come to Heaven?"

"Oh, dear me no," responded Jacob, "but I'll explain that

a little later on."

Then Marty asked, "Am I physically the same as I was on earth?"

"No not really," answered Jacob. "You're an image containing a soul. We've given it the acronym IMCONSO. Your physical matter is left behind when you depart earth, but your image, and we always provide a healthy image, containing your soul rises to Heaven. Your spirit has departed your physical. While here your IMCONSO is loaned speech and thought so we can communicate. In the vernacular you might say your hard copy is left behind and your soft copy proceeds to heaven. More tea?"

"Could you add a couple fingers of Jim Beam?"

As Marty looked around he could see that there were other apparent IMCONSOs being counseled by their blue Mao outfitted acclimators. There were the same looks of bewilderment on their faces as he surely had on his.

"Well," Marty said, "a thousand questions are popping into my mind: where and how do I go on?—will I see family that have gone before me?—do I get to see anyone really important, you know, like Jesus Christ, or maybe even God himself? I certainly don't just sit here in this chair through eternity—tell me that, pray tell me that."

Jacob held up his hands, "Slow down, slow down. I'll respond to your questions, but in a manner we've deemed appropriate. You may, by pure chance, see God. He's awfully busy—He does get, well, all around, you know. Actually you just missed Jesus by a couple of days. He was in our District just a few days ago building us some bookcases for our library—quite a carpenter, as I'm sure you know."

"So I've read."

"Now," went on Jacob, "as to seeing pre-deceased family—probably not, unless they've joined us within the last several months. Now take a sip of tea and I'll tell you why."

Sip.

"Reincarnation."

"REINCARNATION?" Marty about dropped his teacup.

Jacob responded, "More about that later," and went on, "Heaven is governed by the Big Board with, of course, God as Chairman, and then his Board is made up of people, a lot of names which you'd recognize: Moses, Peter, Paul, Mary Magdalene, David, and then some Muslim and other folks who you wouldn't recognize. They're all permanent residents with great responsibilities. Then Heaven is basically divided into Domains determined by the world's great religions: for example Muslim, Buddhism, Jewish, Christian, Hinduism, and the Domains are further sub-divided by Districts with each District having its own Board of Managers. There are three Districts in each Domain where the IMCONSOs are divided as judged upon arrival in Heaven as, Good, Average, Evil. The Good, as implied, are automatically eligible for reincarnation; they go back relatively soon. The Average are eligible, with successful indoctrination, to go back. The Evil can't go back at all and they're all clustered together, in their particular Domain, in the same District 24/7/52 and have to endure terrible wickedness, hate, envy, and jealousy. Imagine for a moment Adolf Hitler and Joseph Stalin discussing forever which one has bragging rights as to, in his relatively short time on earth, who was responsible for the most deaths and destruction. Sorta a hell on Heaven."

Marty wondered, "Are all the Domains alike physically?"

"Well, not exactly, for example if you were to visit the Muslim Domain you'd see the same blue sky, but a lot more sand than grass. As an aside, I occasionally get over there for some administrative duty and when I do I love to put the women in line in front of the men—drives the men nuts. I try and stay outta the Buddhist Domain—that constant droning chanting drive me crazy. You gotta hand it to the Buddists though—they got the reincarnation thing right."

A natural inquiry from Marty, "What about non-believers?"

"Ah, good question with a simple answer—they're in perpetual limbo. That population is really not in my portfolio, but as I understand it the IMCONSOs in limbo do have some sorta ten step program, that if completed, gets them into an appropriate District, but it's not made easy."

Marty challenged, "How did Hitler and Stalin get into the Christian Domain? Seems like they should have been sent to non-believers limbo?"

Jacob responded, "Though it defies reason, Hitler always professed to be a Christian and Stalin may have been lying, but when he got up here he professed to be Russian Orthodox; whatever, they're both worse off in the Christian Evil District than they would have been in non-believers limbo."

Marty wanted to know, "Which religion has it right?"

Jacob responded, "I once asked God which religion was the true religion and He said that was like asking him which was the right road to take to get from Paris to Berlin—He said it makes no difference which road one takes as long as he travels a good road and avoids any serious pot-holes."

"When I go back" Marty asked, "Is my soul reincarnated as a man in America, or could I be an ape in Africa?"

"Oh, you'll be a man. Animals don't have souls because they're just physical matter—they just have a one-way ticket. Now I can't guarantee that if you're reincarnate you'll land in America as it could be anywhere on earth in any situation or circumstance—butcher, baker, candlestick maker. Whatever, if you go back, and you lead a good life, you should have even more cracks at life down below."

"Good, I guess," reacted Marty, "but I'm kinda sorry about the animals though, I won't be seeing my long dead Corky—sure loved that dog."

Marty had to ask, "I don't suppose you have football here?"

To further Marty's enlightenment—"Because people keep going back and forth due to reincarnation there's not as many people in Heaven as you might think—maybe four to five billion. As I said, Heaven is infinite so we really don't get into each others way. As I already suggested, we have permanent and semi-permanent residents here in Heaven.

God's long time loyalists are with him permanently on the Big Board, and, or, acting at the Cabinet level—folks like Moses and the Apostles. The semi-permanent are people for one reason or another God enjoys, or finds helpful, to have around for some indefinite period of time. For example, God was crazy about Will Rogers and kept him around, telling his corny stories, for several years before in went back Frankly I got a little bored with him—same 'ol, same 'ol."

Marty wanted to know, "When does my soul go back and how does it get into another body—does it happen in the womb?"

Patting Marty's hand Jacob said, "In the womb? You'll just have to settle for—we have our ways."

"As to when you'll go back it'll be if and when we feel you're ready, though in most cases it's about a year. What you'll do in the meantime? Probably not too much real exciting, but I promise you enlightenment—you'll read and discuss the classics like *Huckleberry Finn and Moby Dick*; you'll attend philosophical lectures, Schopenhauer and the like, and maybe learn how to play chess. The only nourishment the soul needs is enlightenment. You will pray to God quite a bit; not that He demands adulation, but because you'll come to appreciate and understand fully His gift of life—we really owe Him."

Marty asked, "How long does this go on, that is, the trips back?"

"Well, frankly Marty, after four or five trips back for another life most IMCONSOs have had enough and request eternal rest—you know, enough is enough. You remember before you had your knee replaced you asked your doctor when it would be time to have it done and your doctor told you you'd tell him? It's kinda the same thing; when a IMCONSO has had enough of going back and forth he'll let us know. Of course he doesn't consciously know he's been going back and forth, but unconciously, the soul does."

Jacob said, "Marty there's an Express buggy heading for the interior coming along soon so why don't you catch it and go ahead and enjoy your enlightenment. You'll make new friends and if you've lost family or friends recently there's always the possibility that you'll run in to one or all. There's also a good possibility that you'll run in to one of Jesus' disciples and if you do try and spend some time with them; they have some fantastic stories to tell; particularly Luke— he's a hoot. Don't be afraid to visit with Judas. As biblical scholars on earth have begun to recognize he has been inappropriately maligned—bad rap. I think someone's kidding, but I've heard the only reason he seemed to have a scowl on his face at the Last Supper was because he was expecting a service of whitefish and they served lox—a little levity there Marty."

"Here comes the Express," Jacob said. "Why don't you get aboard and go along to the interior now and I'll hope to see you back here in, maybe a year."

"OK," as Marty boarded the Express along with a half dozen or so other apprehensive IMCONSOs departing for the unknown.

* * *

So, Marty went to inner Heaven doing what people do in Heaven. He learned to play chess, tried but gave up on bridge. He took a couple philosophy courses—Kierkegaard and Sartre—didn't understand a word of it. He inquired about golf, but was told God couldn't tolerate the swearing. He read and participated in discussion groups on the classics. He did run into Luke, who as Jacob had suggested, was quite a character. He had bible study every Tuesday morning. He also met a couple of the other disciples and absorbed their wisdom. He particularly liked Matthew, who he found shared wonderful homilies and would give him all the time he desired. He did run into his cousin Percy who had passed about six months before Marty. He'd choked to death on a fist full of jujubees while at the movies. Marty wasn't particularly fond of Percy, but they had a nice visit.

For levity once a week a traveling stage show came

through Marty's district. He was fortunate enough to see and enjoy the likes of Momma Cass, James Brown, and Patsy Cline. They were semi-permanent residents not considered for early reincarnation because they were in such demand for entertainment in heaven. Their time would eventually come. They say Elvis, however, was in and out.

Marty lost all track of time in Heaven, but was in fact approaching a year when he got word he was to report back to Jacob to get an update on his situation. So, he caught the express buggy back to where it had all started nearly a year before.

Sure enough Jacob was still under the canopy where they had first met and he seemed genuinely pleased to see Marty again.

"Marty, my lad, how good to see you again—as IMCON-SOs go, you're looking well—enjoying your stay?"

"Well," Marty replied, "it's been interesting and I'll have to say, enlightening, but frankly I don't understand all the concentration on enlightenment if it's all ultimately erased when I go back. Seems like it's too late."

"Marty, it stimulates the soul."

"Now, did you meet some interesting people?"

"I sure did—like you warned me, Luke is quite a character. I never knew when he was serious or just pulling my leg."

"Like what?"

"Well, he said the story of Noah and the Ark wasn't exactly true."

"How's that?"

"He says Noah actually had to make several trips."

"And?"

"He said when Moses parted the Red Sea he charged every man, woman, and child a toll and then retired to a villa on Mt. Horeb.

"I think Luke was funning you. Besides, I'll let you in on a little secrete, Moses has lost a little of his luster since the arrival of Charlton Heston."

Marty went on, "I guess my biggest disappointment is that

I never saw God."

Jacob reacted, "Are you sure? Most of the IMCONSOs run into Him sometime or the other when they're here. Do you recall ever seeing a tall slim figure, who appeared nearly opaque, wearing a cloak of swirling wind?"

"Why yes, yes I do, but I thought —

"What?"

"Well, I thought, I thought, that was Morgan Freeman."

"Morgan Freeman!" why he's not even dead yet."

Marty retorted, "In that cloak of swirling wind it sure looked like Morgan Freeman."

"Look Marty, let's talk about your situation and where you go from here. I think I have some good news for you. You're going to be eligible for reincarnation. I have to be candid with you Marty, you weren't a sure thing, being in the Average group and all."

Marty was taken aback, "Average, just average. I thought I'd led a pretty respectable life."

"Ah ha," responded Jacob, "that's the point, pretty respectable, but not extraordinary. In terms of attributes, and I'm overstating to make my point, we don't anticipate any lasting legacies like a school or library named after you. That being said, what you do have is a nice accumulation of good and thoughtful deeds in your portfolio."

"Yeah, like what?" asked a somewhat incredulous Marty.

Jacob responded, "Remember the time several years ago when you were shopping and you noticed a small girl attempting to cash out with a checkerboard in hand, but she was about a dollar and a half short, and you nodded to the store clerk, "go ahead" and unknown to the little girl you covered her shortfall."

"Yeah, I think I remember that—big deal."

"Remember the time you were flying American Airlines and were thumbing through their shopping catalog when you noticed a scale model 737 perched on a pedestal and you recalled that the maintenance man in your building told you how his young son was so enthralled with flying—you clipped the order form and subsequently had a plane sent to the boy anonymously."

"Yes, I do remember that."

"Remember when you anonymously sent the son of a client, who was having financial difficulties, to YMCA camp for two weeks on a presumed scholarship?"

"I'd about forgotten about that."

And Jacob went on, "And there were many other cases of you not looking for accolades or recognition, rather just being kind. Those seemingly little things add up to a significant big thing. On the other hand—"

"NO PLEASE, do we have to go there? I'm fully aware of all my foibles. There's so many things I wished I'd done differently, or not done at all. Not a day goes by that I don't cringe over remembering some stupid thing I'd done in my past. Believe me, I've prayed and asked for forgiveness a multitude of times. I don't know what else I can do."

"Marty, the most important thing you can do is—forgive yourself. Let's move on. You're going back to earth for another crack at it. You'll have to make a trip back to the interior to begin the mechanics of it all—OH,OH, let's move under the canopy, it's starting to rain again and you're getting all wet."

Marty noted, "It sure rains a lot here; it was raining the day I first arrived. I remember that I was—SWOOSH!— SWOOSH!

* * *

Marty, still flat out on the E R table, was now showing encouraging signs of life.

"I'm getting some response—I'm getting some response," exclaimed a nurse.

The bedside equipment was beeping and humming and the light line on the green screen was jumping for joy.

The E R physician excitedly said, "Yea, I'm getting 160 over 93—150 over 90. Hold him steady. I think we're going to pull him through. I'd thought we'd lost him. How long's he been in here—a couple hours?"

"Yea."

"Get word to his wife that it looks like he's going to make it."

"Right."

One of the nurses turned and commented quizzically to the doctor, "How on earth did his hair get so wet? He's soaked."

"Beats me."

Beats all.

END